MAXIM
AND
FYODOR

MAXIM AND FYODOR

AND TWO SHORT STORIES

With illustrations by the author
Translated from the Russian by Andrew Bromfield

VLADIMIR SHINKAREV

SEAGULL PUBLISHING HOUSE LIMITED
LONDON

Published in Great Britain in 2002 by
SEAGULL PUBLISHING HOUSE LIMITED
14 Caterham Road
London SE13 5AR

British Library Cataloguing in Publication Data
A catalogue record for this book is available from
the British Library.

ISBN 0-9543368-0-1

Edited by Gill Rowley
Designed and typeset by Price Watkins Design
Printed and bound in Great Britain
by The St Edmundsbury Press Ltd, Bury St. Edmunds, Suffolk.
Distributed by BBR Distribution

CONTENTS

With special thanks to David

A BOOK OF ITS TIME

Vladimir Shinkarev was born in 1954 in Leningrad, now (once again) St Petersburg, and is therefore a member of an artistic generation that reached maturity and early middle age under communism and has remained creatively active under the new conditions of post-communist democratic Russia.

Well-known as a painter, he has been exhibited widely in Europe and the USA, notably at the UN headquarters in New York in 2000 and at the Art 2002 festival in London. In Russia his fame as an artist is inextricably linked with his leading role in the artists' group Mitki, established during the 1980s. His visual art has been described as a synthesis of the continuing elite cultural tradition of St Petersburg and his own version of pop-art and modernism, incorporating a wide range of different sources and motifs.

But in Russia Shinkarev is also a writer of considerable fame, and like his painting his writing combines a refined cultural sensibility with elements of primitivism, the absurd and emphatic humour. He has described himself, a typical St Petersburger, in the following terms: "I suffer from a stomach ulcer and a heart defect. I have the gloomy character of a boorish swine. In that kind of mood you can't write anything coarse and loutish. Somehow it all turns out subtle and psychological."

Shinkarev's fame as a writer is also directly linked with the Mitki group. As Andrei Bitov expresses it, although the various members of this remarkable drinking brotherhood of painters possessed a range of talents, Shinkarev was the only one with the gift of the word. The image of the Mitki was floating in the air, but it still had to be invented. Shinkarev did this in his writing.

Shinkarev's group manifesto *The Mitki* posited a mass youth movement embodying the life-style of his artistic milieu in a way that made everyone believe it already existed, and thereby effectively brought it into existence. The philosophy of this milieu is explored in *Maxim and Fyodor*, written in 1980. The book was banned under communism, but became a best-seller in the 1990s, has been published in translation in Poland and Germany, and is now in print in Italy.

Clearly, the fact that Shinkarev's writing was officially banned did not mean that nobody read it: quite the opposite, in fact. *Maxim and Fyodor* became one of those books that is lived by a generation, passing beyond mere cult status to become contemporary folk myth. The Russian youth of the 1980s and 1990s repeatedly plundered Shinkarev's manifesto *The Mitki* for catchphrases, so that the language of his prose had a significant impact on colloquial spoken usage, the folk language of the street and kitchen.

Both *The Mitki* and *Maxim and Fyodor* are canonical texts in a distinctive Russian popular/underground tradition which in Soviet times includes the satirical classics *The Twelve Chairs* and *The Golden Calf* and the absurdist writings of the Oberiuty group, but which extends back into pre-revolutionary times via the abstruse philosophical ponderings of Kozma Prutkov. One of the eminent precursors of *Maxim and Fyodor* in this line is another book with a heavily alcoholic bias, *Moscow-Petushki* by Veniamin Erofeev.

Erofeev's work, which receives an honourable mention in the present book in the chapter "Thus Spake Maxim", depicts the ethos of the Soviet '60s – a time when people could still think that Soviet life might be going somewhere – through the metaphor of a train journey. Anyone seeking understanding of the changed Soviet life of the 1970s could hardly find a better starting place than *Maxim and Fyodor*, which heartened and encouraged those who were no longer waiting for life to begin, and did not want to carry on *not living*. This apparently disparate series of vignettes set within a subtle conceptual framework is crammed with significant detail and psychological nuances that succinctly convey the essential quality of life at the time as seen from within by a 26-year-old working, in the best traditions of the Soviet intelligentsia, in a boiler room.

Under the conditions of Soviet ideology, censorship and *samizdat*, a concern for creative freedom naturally focused on its inner dimension, and the works which nourished a sense of inner freedom became literary monuments. The important role played by Zen Buddhism in

Maxim and Fyodor is therefore both a reflection of a real historical fact and a metaphor for the role of such literature in the life of the time. Similarly, while alcoholism is central to the social insight and humour of *Maxim and Fyodor* this is not a book that glorifies drunkenness as such. Its true theme is freedom and creativity, the vital life of the spirit (alchohol provides the freedom necessary for creation, but in a different country and different circumstances its place could be taken by something else).

In this early work Shinkarev indulges freely in literary brilliance and, of course, humour. The two other stories included in this volume, *The Tame Hedgehog* (1987) and *The King of the Beasts* (1998), demonstrate an increasing movement away from the boisterous rebellion of youth to mature concern with the simple expression of insight and wisdom. The Tolstoyan intonations of *Hedgehog* are overtly emphasised by the offering of a choice between two unhappy endings. In *The King of the Beasts* the prose (and the mood) has been stripped of the final traces of embellishment. But the development throughout, from riotous exuberance to meditative calm, is underpinned by the same seriousness of intent. In parallel manner, the transition of the members of the Mitki group from drunkenness to sobriety under democracy, including Shinkarev's own development from alcoholic artist to apologist for Alcoholics Anonymous, signifies a new twist in the spiral of freedom when, as Andrei Bitov puts it, drunkenness ceased to be a form of independence and became a form of dependence, i.e. of voluntary unfreedom.

The society that was the Soviet Union in the 1970s and the position of the artist within that society may have changed in many ways, but however deeply rooted *Maxim and Fyodor* may be in that time, its compound of wit and pathos seems to have retained the vital power to entertain and amuse.

Andrew Bromfield

MAXIM AND FYODOR

A work of three parts

Everything seemed strange to him in this
world, created as though for some fast-moving,
mocking game. But this deliberately arranged
game has dragged on for ages, for an eternity,
and no one feels like laughing any more, they
can't . . .
Inside, these poor creatures carry the sense of a
different, happy role, indispensable and essential
– why are they so oppressed and expectant?

Andrei Platonov

PART ONE

MAXIM AND FYODOR

THOUGHTS
(aphorisms, maxims, fyodors)

Maxim alone denied the greatness of the philosophy of Marxism. However, when he was summoned to that other place, he denied his own denial there, becoming convinced thereby of the validity of the law of the contradiction of the contradiction.

* * *

Maxim scorned his friend Fyodor's political illiteracy and low intellectual capacity and was fond of stressing that he and his friend were complete opposites. Not infrequently this issue caused them to become embroiled in vituperation or even brawling. On one occasion, after lamping Fyodor good and hard, Maxim was gratified to note that he had mastered the law of the unity and struggle of opposites.

* * *

Ever since he was a child, Maxim's friend Pyotr (concerning whom we shall hear in greater detail later) had suffered from an irresistible urge to commit suicide. When walking over a bridge, he was frequently unable to resist the temptation to settle his scores with life, and he would throw himself off. After coming to his senses, Pyotr would then swim the rest of the way.

The suicidal moods that overwhelmed the impressionable youth thus provided him with excellent physical training and helped him acquire the physique of a professional sportsman.

In commenting on this fact, Maxim would refer with gratitude to the law of the transformation of quantity into quality, which should not be dismissed lightly.

* * *

Maxim soon developed such a powerful grasp of the philosophy of Marxism that he found no difficulty in devising new immutable laws of the development of human society.

Thus, when gazing upon his friend Fyodor, Maxim would often say, completely off the cuff as he polished off the second bottle of port: "Like is dissimilar to like!"

* * *

Maxim had so many powerful thoughts that it's hard to single any out. For instance, he was often visited by a thought of quite exceptional power: "Where can I borrow 25 roubles?"

* * *

It sometimes happened that Fyodor was also able to teach Maxim a thing or two. For instance, one day Maxim gave Fyodor a book to read (one of those that are best not discussed with people you don't know very well). Fyodor went off down to the boulevard to read, but he fell into a daydream, had a beer or two, and failed to notice that he'd misplaced the book.

"Where's the book, then?" Maxim enquired that evening.

"I've lost it," Fyodor replied.

Maxim showered Fyodor with abuse, but the latter struck back by asking: "What's up, was it a good book?"

Maxim merely gnashed his teeth in reply. Then Fyodor declaimed Nekrasov's immortal lines:

Broadcast the wise, the good and the eternal!
Sow these seeds and Russia's folk will render you
Its heartfelt gratitude!

Not knowing what retort to make to that, Maxim could only continue to gnash his teeth.

* * *

Maxim was capable of sacrificing anything on the altar of thought, even the most essential of items.

One day he said: "When I think that beer is made up of atoms, it puts me right off drinking it."

* * *

Maxim's friend Pyotr loved to indulge in discourse along the lines of everything being possible for man, and so forth.

Maxim heard out these deliberations in sullen silence, then declared in true Aesopean style: "Try drinking out of a colander then!" and left the room, slamming the door behind him.

* * *

Having observed that Maxim was drinking without taking anything to eat, Fyodor enquired whether this might be because he had recalled the molecular and atomic structure of the hors d'oeuvres.

Maxim proudly shook his head and said: "He who does not work, neither shall he eat!"

* * *

A certain remark is ascribed to Maxim, although this is not authenticated.

When he was hung-over, Fyodor would launch into an interminable narrative about drinking partners of his who had disappeared, or about the time when he used to go to school, or about some villages or other. As he rambled on, Fyodor would lapse into long silences, sometimes restricting himself to nothing but interjections or gestures for as long as five minutes.

If Pyotr didn't leave immediately, he suffered agonies of boredom and slouched about the room, interrupting Fyodor with his own escapist romantic fantasies.

Observing Pyotr's positive dislike of Fyodor's narratives, Maxim said: "Not even a work of literature can be judged by the words it contains."

A GARDEN OF STONES
(haikus, tankas, armoured cars)

Maxim follows a path between steep rocks.
Reaching a cherry tree in bloom,
He halted, choking on his tears.

* * *

Fyodor awoke with a fierce hangover,
Beneath a Japanese garden's blooming cherry.
He weeps, not knowing how he came here.

* * *

Fyodor staggers towards
The local railway station.
Shaking his head,
He stares at the timetable:
Mikasa, Kasuga, Kyoto,
Avadza, Inamidzuma
And distant Tago Bay.
What of it? With just such despair
He used to stare and see:
Ryabovo, Rzhevka, Griva,
Piskaryovka, Vsevolozhsk
And distant Petrokrepost.
Icy malice of the platforms.

* * *

A swan felled on the wing, Fyodor slumped across a flowering
cherry,
When Maxim lamped him smack between the ears.

* * *

Maxim walked down the path.
Fyodor approached.
Maxim knocked him aside.
"Why d'you go shoving me?"
Fyodor cried out, offended.
"Why d'you lumber on like a tank?"
Was Maxim's calm reply to him.

* * *

Desiring to research the glass-clinking phenomenon,
Maxim and Fyodor took a jug of sake
And laboured stubbornly through day and night.
Next day they rose,
Their heads like sour and sweaty armoured cars.

* * *

Fyodor sat many hours in a stone garden,
Waiting there for Maxim.
Maxim was seeking sake in the shops.

* * *

Maxim stood with his finger raised.
Fyodor laughed.
Thus did they both master the core of Zen.

* * *

A Japanese friend brought a jug of sake
And told Maxim and Fyodor with a civil smile
To bring sakura-cherries for hors d'oeuvres.

But they, their knowledge of his language less than perfect,
Instead of sakura bring him a chicken.

* * *

Fyodor mastered the Japanese life-style.
And though a bed was where he slept before,
After carousing with his Japanese friends
He slumped straight down on to the matting,
Lacking the strength to crawl back to his bed.

* * *

Daydreaming, Fyodor sat beneath a cherry's shade,
Set down before him great Ransetsu's tome,
Took out his shag and tore a page out for a roll-up.
Finding no pictures there, he tossed the book aside,
Withdrawing into inward contemplation.

* * *

Mount Fuji slowly creeps out of the fog.
Maxim and Fyodor walk across its slope,
Embracing, heads inclined against each other . . .
If only they had Hokusai here now!

* * *

Like spray above a foaming brook, this cherry blossom.
Maxim and Fyodor sit upon the slender bridge.
An emerald glint of jasper flashes bright between them,
A bottle focusing the streaming rays of light.
The happy seasonal coolness of the spring.

* * *

Maxim harassed his pupil Pyotr with hard work,
Making him tidy up and take the bottles back.
He made him commit hara-kiri all the time.

* * *

In classical culture
Maxim could thrash young Pyotr like a little boy.
He smashed his face with Hokusai
And walloped him
With two volumes of Akutagava.

A JAPANESE DANCE

The sun did rise behind Mount Fuji's peak.
Geese floated down the river.
Maxim to Fyodor he did say:
"Get down there to that shop."

* * *

Fyodor sucked on the bottle greedily
And it was emptied in a trice.
Maxim knew not if he should laugh or cry.

* * *

Grieving is not eternal – lo, the east glows red,
The tribe of traders hastens to its shops,
The sake-seller takes his padlock down,
Yawns, covering his mouth up with his hand,
And Fyodor, standing on the narrow porch,
Cries out to him: "Banzai! Banzai!"

* * *

Finding Fyodor sunk deep in meditation,
Maxim, not wishing to disturb his friend,
Drank the house dry before he went to bed.
On waking he repented to observe
That Fyodor's sleeves were soaking wet from tears.

* * *

All is concealed by night.
The breakers seethe unseen.
Trembling, Maxim drinks water in the kitchen.

THERE AND BACK AGAIN
(Zen Buddhist fables and koans)

One morning Maxim, being mightily hung-over, sat cradling his head
in his hands and rocking from side to side.

Fyodor approached him and asked the following question: "What
is the meaning of Buddhism?"

"Go stick your Buddhism up your arse!" Maxim exclaimed feebly.
Confounded, Fyodor withdrew.

* * *

A certain youth by the name of Pyotr, on hearing of the philosophical
prowess of Maxim, with whom he was as yet unacquainted, came to
his house and addressed Fyodor, whom he mistakenly took to be
Maxim, with the following question: "What is the meaning of the
advent of the Bodhisattva of the south?"

After pondering a while, Fyodor calmly replied: "Dunno."

At that point Maxim intervened in the discussion, saying: "Fuck
off and stick your Bodhisattva up your arse!"

Confounded, Pyotr withdrew, glorifying Maxim and Fyodor.

* * *

Another youth, Vasilii, apprised by Pyotr of what had come to pass,
came to Maxim and Fyodor and sought the advice of the latter as to
whether or not he should enter a monastery. Fyodor kneaded a *papyros* in his fingers and said nothing.

Maxim intervened in the discussion, saying: "Go fuck yourself!"

Thus enlightened, Vasilii could not tell which reply was the better
of the two.

* * *

The novice Vasilii presented Fyodor with Daisetsu Suzuki's book *Zen Living*. Fyodor asked Maxim what he should do with this gift.

"Hang it in the crapper for all I care," replied Maxim.

And so the enlightened Fyodor did.

* * *

One day Fyodor enquired of Maxim: "What is the meaning of Zen Buddhism?"

Maxim looked at Fyodor and fetched him a wallop across his bad ear.

Unable to restrain himself, Fyodor replied with a blow to the bread-basket. Maxim controlled the pain and continued the lesson by poking Fyodor in the eye and giving him another clout for good measure, and when Fyodor turned to go he booted him up the backside. Fyodor withdrew.

* * *

One night Fyodor, woken by a powerful hangover, greatly desired to drink. Without switching on the light, he went through to the kitchen, felt along the shelf for a bottle and began drinking. After taking his first swallow, he realised he was in error and the bottle did not contain water, as he had supposed, but kerosene.

However, so powerful was Fyodor's mastery of Zen Buddhism that he discovered within himself the courage not to rectify his error and calmly finished the entire bottle.

* * *

When he was drunk, Fyodor liked to play with the cat. One morning, having woken with a bad hangover, he discovered that in his previous day's sport he had stuffed the cat into an empty glass jar from which the creature could not possibly be extracted. Of course, it would have been a shame to break the jar.

However, his lessons in Zen Buddhism had not been in vain. Hitting upon the correct solution without a moment's thought, Fyodor handed in the jar for the money with the cat still in it.

* * *

When Fyodor experienced *satori*, he would shout out in his great joy. The other people in the flat often rebuked him for this shouting, and one day they wrote a complaint to the housing management office. A notice arrived from the housing management office with an invitation to attend the people's court.

Fyodor enquired of Maxim what he should do with the notice.

"Wipe your arse with it for all I care" was Maxim's reply.

And that was what Fyodor did.

* * *

Lying at the entrance to Maxim and Fyodor's house was a great chunk of wood.

Every time he walked past it, Fyodor would say: "Just look at that chunk!"

On one occasion Maxim's pupil Pyotr exclaimed: "Do you have to say that every time? I can see it's a chunk!"

Maxim, walking beside Pyotr, raised his fist to his pupil's nose and said: "But have you seen this?"

Confounded, Pyotr realised what was what and beat it.

* * *

Pyotr noticed that Fyodor had a strange habit: having waited his turn in a long queue at the beer stall, at the last moment he would leave without buying any beer, although it cost him an obvious effort. Pyotr enquired as to why Fyodor did this, when five minutes later he would come back and stand in the queue again anyway.

Fyodor replied steadfastly: "If a created work is to dwell in eternity, it should not be taken to its conclusion."

Pyotr struck himself on the forehead and retired.

* * *

"Then drink out of a colander!" Maxim declared in reply to Pyotr's boastful claims that everything was supposedly possible for man and so forth.

Confounded, Pyotr did so.

* * *

"What is there left for a man to do when the noose has already been put round his neck?" Maxim enquired.

"The sakura is beautiful not only when in blossom," Pyotr blurted out with his characteristic elegance.

In place of a reply Vasilii took a box of matches and dropped it on the floor, and although matchboxes do not break when they fall on the floor, the clatter woke Fyodor, who muttered in his drowsiness: "Whassa? Where am I?. . . What?"

As always, Maxim acknowledged his reply to be the best.

* * *

Here is an account of an incident that is highly dubious, but even such information concerning Maxim and Fyodor is not to be despised.

Maxim once enquired what, in Pyotr's opinion, was the meaning of Zen.

"Zen," said Pyotr, a devotee of elegant but dim-witted similes, "is the ability to pour two full glasses of vodka from a quarter bottle."

"From an empty bottle," Vasilii chimed in.

Maxim transferred his gaze to Fyodor.

"And not drink the vodka," stated Fyodor.

Gratified, Maxim nodded and said: "And not pour it into glasses."

MAXIM MONOGATARI

1

There was once a man by the name of Maxim. And one day, so they say, he said to the lady who worked behind the counter in the Vodka and Spirits shop:

The heartening glow
Of green and lovely herbs
Is now become oblivion's juice . . .
And like a swine –
I'll come back for another!

The salesgirl, however, said nothing in reply, merely taking a bottle of Hunter's Herbal vodka out of the crate and holding it out to him.

2

Once upon a time Maxim happened to say to the lady who worked behind the counter in the Vodka and Spirits shop:

Though Cleopatra in the flesh
Should be my own true love,
Her ardent hands
Could scarcely fire me with such passion
As your elegant and heedless wave.

In reply the salesgirl wiped down a bottle and set it on the counter in front of Maxim, but said nothing; perhaps she hadn't understood or hadn't heard him properly – I cannot tell.

3

There was at one time a cavalier by the name of Maxim. And it happened one day that he said to the salesgirl in the wine section of the Delicatessen:

The brief days of our life rush hurtling by,
Their pace astoundingly impetuous,
Like current running through electric wires.
Fair lady, are not you the lofty pole
Raising that wire above the lowly ground?

It is possible that the lady might have answered him, but it was not to be, for another cavalier by the name of Pyotr, happening to be present, hastened to proclaim, and no doubt with good reason:

Most truly have you spoken here
Of the astounding pace of passing days,
Like unto current in electric wires
Which draw support from pillars such as this.
Without support the wire would break.

And so the two cavaliers, both praising and exalting this fair lady, waited not on her reply and set out quickly from the shop for home.

4

Once there were three cavaliers. The first cavalier bore the name of Maxim. The second cavalier bore the name of Fyodor. The third cavalier bore the name of Pyotr. One day the cavalier Pyotr leapt up from the table at which all three were sitting, wrapped a scarf around his neck and chest and set out briskly for the Delicatessen, evidently in order to see the lady who worked as a salesgirl in the wine section. And on seeing that the Delicatessen was open and that the lady was standing behind the counter, he drew a deep breath and said (for how well the young men could say things in those times!):

Indeed, Maxim did not speak idly
Of our brief life's astounding days
Of lofty poles and humming wires,
Resounding to the earth's own song.
And higher yet the clouds are ringing.

The lady made no reply; she had evidently failed to realise that Pyotr wished to explain to her the happy impossibility of gathering the whole of life into your fist.

5

The renowned cavalier Fyodor, walking through a courtyard to keep a tryst with a fair lady, staggered and stepped into some sewage and composed a verse about it:

I was walking to a date,
But I stepped into this shit.

6

Once upon a time not so very long ago it happened that the two cavaliers Maxim and Pyotr were standing in the queue at the beer kiosk and one of them, Pyotr in fact, began bemoaning his wasted life, or perhaps he took a serious dislike to the yard in which the kiosk stood, I cannot tell, but the words he spoke were these:

Steering his fragile bark across the strait
Someone is sailing fearlessly,
Intrepid, heart a-blaze within his breast
Sea-spray a-gleaming on his knee-boots.
But here is only beery froth and mud . . .

Maxim made him answer:

> *But here is only beery froth and mud,*
> *Yet learn to look beyond the swirling mist,*
> *And you will see, with valour writ upon our brow,*
> *How we do sail across a foaming gulf,*
> *The sea-spray wispy on our gleaming boots.*

On hearing this, Pyotr stamped his feet and wept in rapture, and few were those in the queue who could restrain their tears, some even fell upon the ground and lay in the mud, singing loud songs, and only the lady selling the beer said nothing – perhaps she was too agitated, or perhaps she did not quite catch what was said.

7

One day the cavalier by the name of Maxim spoke as follows to the lady who was selling draught beer in a kiosk:

> *How can the shore be parted from the wave?*
> *Or Fuji parted from its snow?*
> *You saw me here but yesterday*
> *You'll see me here again today, tomorrow.*
> *How can the sun be parted from its rays?*

On hearing this, all who were standing around the kiosk burst into tears, and so fine were these lines that after them no other verses were recited in the queue.

FOR THE PEOPLE'S CAUSE
(a black-and-white silent film scenario)

Blackout.

Titles.

Blackout.

Camera pans across Leningrad. The Peter and Paul Fortress in the rays of the setting sun. A cloud-covered sky. Rousing music plays to musical accompaniment.

Blackout.

Title: PETROGRAD. THE BEGINNING OF THE TWENTIETH CENTURY

Blackout.

A room. Morning.

Standing in the centre of the room is a battered table with a table-cloth pulled halfway off it. Standing and lying on the table and under it are bottles, glasses, dirty plates and cigarette butts.

Camera pans round the room. A chest, a cupboard, an oleograph of Repin's *Volga Boatmen*, an ottoman. Two people are sleeping on the ottoman under padded jackets and rags.

Title: MORNING FINDS MAXIM AND FYODOR AT A FRIEND'S APARTMENT.

Camera fades in on the ottoman. Fyodor throws aside his padded jacket, stands up and looks around uneasily. He goes over to the table, pokes at the plates with his fingers and moves away. He wanders aimlessly round the room a few times, frequently stopping and listening for something. It is clear from the way Fyodor moves and the expression on his face that he badly needs to go to the toilet, but he is too embarrassed to go looking for it in an unfamiliar apartment. He goes over to the door and opens it cautiously. After a while he closes it just as cautiously. He goes across to the ottoman, sits down beside the sleeping Maxim and lights up a cigarette. The camera focuses for a long time on Fyodor smoking and Maxim lying under the rags.

Smoke drifts around the room. Outside the window there is fog.

(The cheerlessness of the shot is reminiscent of the episode in Carnet's film *Daybreak* when a tear-gas grenade is thrown in through the window of the hero's room.) Fyodor gets up, goes across to the table and pokes at the plates with his fingers. He goes to the window. We can see Fyodor's hunched figure and part of the room.

The previously invisible cover of an underground cellar suddenly opens, flinging dust up into the air. A tremor runs down Fyodor's back; a small stream of urine runs out of his trouser leg and trickles across the floor. About twenty underground activists with steadfast, resolute faces emerge from the trapdoor.

Paying no attention to the petrified Fyodor, the underground activists walk quickly towards the door. They move in such a dense, unified mass that it seems as though some large animal like a seal is crawling from the underground cellar to the door. Some of the underground activists are very tall, and some of them are so small that they mince along under the coat-tails of the others.

After the underground activists leave the room, Fyodor stands without moving for about three minutes, then he dashes over to the window, lifts up the lace curtain and gazes out avidly.

View from the window: the group of underground activists moves away down the street, brushing bystanders aside.

Fyodor dashes across to the ottoman, shoves and shakes the sleeping Maxim. Close up: Fyodor's face, highly agitated, yelling something.

Title: MAXIM! MAXIM! WAKE UP! FOR GOD'S SAKE WAKE UP! I SAW THE UNDERGROUND ACTIVISTS! THEY WERE FIGHTING FOR THE PEOPLE'S CAUSE!

Maxim turns over. His face is dark and angry. Raising his head slightly, he says something and lies back down again, pulling the padded jacket up over his head.

Title: GO STICK YOUR UNDERGROUND ACTIVISTS UP YOUR ARSE!

Blackout.

Title: THE END.

THE LAY OF MY MAXIM
(an epic poem in 24 tirades)

1

That morn did Fyodor rise betimes
And go into the kitchen.
Standing there
Were bottles five of Zhigulyovskoe,
Five of Martovskoe
And five of Admiralty too,
With various other beers a-plenty.

2

Day was dawning.
On the board its bright rays limned
The bottles' elegant forms,
Their lines rousing the mind, pleasing the eye,
Prompting the ominous recall
Of Gaudí's masterworks.

3

Immune to terror or reproach,
Fyodor
Seized on a bottle of Zhiguli
And whacked it like a sword across the table's edge.
Off flew the cap, the beer poured forth.
The cat beneath the board reclining
Began to lap the beer up with a lingering moan.

4

The world was still
As Fyodor stood in bugler's pose.
The muscles of his mighty neck moved up and down.

5

Finishing one,
Fyodor took up another,
And deftly flicked the cap off with his nail.
The beer gushed strongly as a fountain
And Fyodor caught it in his trembling lips,
Waving his arms and laughing like a child.

6

But half-way through he halted,
Standing long in silence grave,
Attending to some inward sense.
Out through the window did he peer
With an eagle's
Piercing gaze.

7

A bloodshot hoop drifted
                    above the pallid town.
Through putrid yards and tedious building sites
The fog streamed on,
Seeking to sweep away
The ugly works of nature's lords.

8

The fog was wonderfully thick . . .
And Fyodor,
Strain his keen eyes as he might,
Could not descry that which
He wished to see –
He could not see the beer kiosk.

9

Stubborn of wit was Fyodor,
But lacking wisdom.
Divining not nature's true outward form,
He thought the stall had been demolished in the night.

10

However,
Driving woe's lines from his brow,
Fyodor
Grasped yet his beer with doughty hand
And drained it,
Opened another and drank that,
And then supped beers many and various,
Until a seeming shot alarmed his ear.
Affrighted, Fyodor fell,
Although he was not of the timid tribe.

11

But what had happened?
'Twas Maxim,
Op'ning a bottle with his steadfast hand,
Who, mightily hung o'er, mistook his strength,
Let drop the bottle and himself collapsed,
And like a pistol shot the shock resounded.

12

Like to a fallen knight
Maxim did lie, his arms proudly outspread.
Like to the victim of a glorious and guiltless death
Was Fyodor, lying at his side.
The cat, with dismal mien, stood some way off
Like to a raven on the field of battle.

13

But Fyodor rose,
Knitting his brows,
And strove to fathom this event.
Maxim stood up, badmouthing Fyodor,
Threatening fearsome vengeance
For something or other.

14

Witting not his own guilt, Fyodor,
Grasping a Martovskoe,
*   did smoothly wrench away*
The cap clenched in his teeth,
But did not drink,
Gallantly proffering the bottle to Maxim,

Who haughtily did spurn this gift,
And took a bottle of his own
To open with a table knife,
Wounding himself full sore, 'tis true,
And spilling almost all the beer.

15

Supping on what remained, Maxim
                produced a pack of Belomor
And flicked it from below
As mightily as Pushkin's Balda might have flicked.
And flying out, a papyros
Fell in the beery puddle and was drenched.

16

Maxim flicked once again,
Took out a papyros
And forcibly did blow into its tube.
His mighty breath, in unrestrainèd vigour,
Blasted all the tobacco from within.

17

Then, soft'ning skilfully a pair of papyroses,
Fyodor smiled brightly as he gave Maxim a light.

18

A sudden scorching smell.
The cat screeched vilely,
Hurtled into the pool of beer
And rolled around there.
Fyodor had dropped his match on to the cat.

19

Heartily did the two friends laugh at this.
Fyodor, to mark the reconciliation,
Two Martovskoe beers took up,
Linked them and pulled,
Op'ning them both,
So skilled was he in this!

20

Meanwhile, the fog dispersing,
The crimson orb of day
Slid on along its arc
As though it would have shunned that squalid land.

21

The friends drank up
And set the bottles down,
Taking up fresh ones filled with Admiralty beer.
His draught yet uncompleted,
Maxim went off to urinate.

22

On his return
He tipped the bottle back
And set it to his ever-thirsting lips,
But thereupon did snort
And set it down again.

23

For it transpired
That while Maxim was urinating
Fyodor with vodka strong had topped his bottle up.
Maxim laughed hearty at this noble jest,
Confessed that Fyodor
Had grown strong in wit,
And in token of his true goodwill
Drank down the mix, unfearing,
To the end.

24

And much there was that happened after that,
But let me end my epic story here,
The reason of its writing now exhausted.
This morning was I gasping for a beer,
But have o'ercome the lusting through my art.

FINITA LA TRAGEDIA
(a tragedy)

ACT ONE

The heavy yellow-green curtain rises. The scene is set in Maxim and Fyodor's room. Maxim is sleeping on a badly sagging camp bed. His face is dark and angry. Hanging above the camp bed are reproductions and photographs cut from the magazines *Awakening* and *The Sun of Russia*. A table is set centre-stage. On the table and under it there are dirty plates, empty and half-empty bottles, cigarette butts, a few glasses. Fyodor is sitting at the table, sunk deep in thought. A cat runs around the stage.

Fyodor pours himself a glass of wine and downs it in a single gulp. His head slumps forward on to his chest. He doesn't move. He is obviously falling asleep. The entire stage is a vision of oppressive gloom. The vulgarity of Fyodor's movements is unpleasant, the way he reaches for a bottle, overturning all the glasses and plates in his way.

The whole thing, from the very beginning, begins to seem like a terrible load of old rubbish.

Meanwhile absolutely nothing happens on stage for forty-five minutes, after which the curtain falls.

ACT TWO

The curtain rises and everything on the stage is still the same. Forty-five minutes go by.

The spectators begin to think they've stumbled into an avant-garde production and they'll be shown Maxim and Fyodor sleeping all the way to the end; but suddenly the middle ground of the stage is lit up and the events that take place there are so intensely absorbing that those members of the audience who have not yet left the theatre are certain to feel their patience has been well rewarded.

This is a sight to behold.

The action on the mid-plane of the stage involves numerous characters, the reason for the presence of some of whom is a mystery.

They are:

> the spirit of Maxim,
> the spirit of Fyodor,
> the spirit of Pyotr,
> the spirit of Vasilii,
> the spirits of their Japanese friends,
> the spirits of various elegant ladies, including:
>> the spirit of the salesgirl from the wine
>> section and
>> the spirit of the salesgirl from the beer kiosk
>> (and why not?
>> What's wrong with them?),
> the spirits of the other people from the apartment,
> the spirits of the underground activists,
> the spirits of bystanders from the street,
> the spirit of I. Konstantinov,
> the spirit of Hokusai,
> the spirit of Ransetsu,
> the spirit of Daisetsu Suzuki,
> the spirit of Antonio Gaudì,
> the spirit of Alexander Pushkin,

and also many other spirits up to and including the spirits of the spectators in the theatre.

The bizarre sight of the interaction of these spirits is hard to describe.

Some of the spirits can see all, or almost all, of the other spirits, some can only see some of the others, some can only see themselves, and there are some spirits who are not even sure of their own existence. It is amusing that certain spirits can only see certain parts of their own bodies, and probably of the other spirits too, such as a clenched fist, with which they lash out at anything and everything.

Equally unpleasant are the spirits who cannot see anything at all: they stroll briskly around the stage, painfully shunting the others aside.

Despite all the rumpus and hullabaloo, it is clear that the sleeping Maxim and Fyodor are the focus of many of the spirits' attention. Some regard them with scorn, some with indignation, some with pity, some with laughter, some with understanding, some with curiosity, and in all sorts of other ways. The spirit of Maxim and the spirit of Fyodor regard them with an indeterminate expression.

The middle ground of the stage starts gradually fading into darkness. One by one the spirits disappear and the hubbub subsides. The last to disappear are the spirits of Maxim and Fyodor, and in the silence that descends we can hear their final enigmatic comments.

Spirit of Maxim: He is waking.

Spirit of Fyodor: But not . . .

(The mid-plane of the stage is in darkness. Fyodor raises his head. The yellow-green curtain descends, but before it conceals the stage completely we see Fyodor reaching out for a bottle.)

PART TWO

RETURN FROM JAPAN

BLOW-UP

On the one hand Ilya Davidovich Kobot was not fond of his flat-mates Maxim and Fyodor. He even wrote complaints about them, saying that Fyodor yelled and shouted in the middle of the night, that they brought in drinking companions and pissed in the corridor and the kitchen, but on the other hand they do say most neighbours are worse than they were . . . Fyodor was such a wretched creature, he'd never insult you to your face, and Maxim might be as stroppy as a sergeant-major, but he spent most of the time sleeping.

One evening Kobot was sitting in their room drinking tea – you have to take a look at how other people live every now and then. And a fine choice he'd made of whom to take a look at . . . he should have left right at the beginning. From the very beginning they started swearing at each other: first Maxim abused Fyodor roundly for buying vermouth when there was port in the shop, then he abused him again for fiddling with the beer – he kept opening the top of the bottle and then popping it back on again.

And that evening Fyodor kept sticking a disgusting word he'd learned from the novice Vasilii into every phrase he spoke – the word "pantheism". For instance: "Right then, how about another glass of pantheism?" – that was about the vermouth. Or else: "I've drunk a pantheistic amount of beer today!" Kobot left the room specially to look the word up in the *Soviet Encyclopaedic Dictionary* and it wasn't there!

They went on sitting there, mostly not saying anything, when suddenly the door opened and they saw a militiaman standing in the doorway.

Come to think of it, who was it opened the front door for him?

Of course, Kobot got a very bad fright, but it was clear enough the militiaman hadn't come for him. Most likely it was Fyodor he was interested in. Maxim was angry enough before, but now he went all black in the face – he suspected Fyodor too, thinking: "Right, you asshole, no more yelling and shouting in the middle of the night!" Fyodor himself didn't really grasp the situation: "What's going on? Whassee doin' 'ere?"

The militiaman looked them all over with a sullen eye, resting it on Fyodor in particular, and asked: "Which of you's Kobot?"

Kobot's heart began pounding painfully, and the torment of being embarrassed in front of Maxim and Fyodor was still worse. The miserable drunkards were actually looking at him in sympathy.

"I'm . . . Kobot . . ."

"Well hello, Kobot," the militiaman said after a pause, removing his peaked cap.

"Hello . . ."

Kobot got to his feet and stood to attention. Maxim took a couple of bottles of vermouth off the table and stood them on the floor. The militiaman transferred his inquisitive glance from Kobot to Maxim: "Do you live here too?"

"Yes," Fyodor replied calmly, "pantheistically."

"Well then, hello to you too. I'm going to be your new flat-mate, Alexei Stepanovich Puzhaty."

What with this unexpected turn of events and the accursed uproar in his heart, Kobot was streaming with sweat and his legs were trembling. He staggered across to the door in a long curve, not noticing the militiaman's stare of amazement.

"What's up with him? Sick, is he?" Puzhaty asked.

"He's an asshole," Maxim replied after a brief delay, downing half a glass of vermouth.

* * *

The new tenant settled into the apartment quickly, on the very first day in fact. In the morning, when Kobot was putting the kettle on, lively whistling broke out in the corridor and Puzhaty erupted into the kitchen in his vest.

"Hi there!" he said in a loud voice.

"Good morning," replied Kobot. He'd prepared the phrase in advance, to say it to the militiaman – he knew he would be very embarrassed after what happened the day before and wouldn't be able to think of anything to say straight away.

"Why'd you clear off like that yesterday? Frightened or something, were you?"

Kobot blushed, not knowing how to answer.

"What's up? Cat got your tongue?"

Kobot fumbled with the gas without speaking, but he couldn't get it to light. Puzhaty lit the gas on his ring, put his kettle on and began watching Kobot's fumbling.

"Where d'you work?"

"I work at the Mechanical . . ." Kobot answered after a pause for thought.

"What, what? How's that?"

"That's what they call it."

An awkward silence ensued. Kobot, having made such an effort to switch on the gas, switched it off and went back to his room. Once inside, he walked rapidly to and fro like the day before, his head empty of thoughts.

* * *

That evening as he was coming home from work and already getting close to the apartment block, Kobot saw Puzhaty standing in the doorway and instinctively, without even thinking about it, turned away with a shudder and walked on past the building.

"Hey, Kobot!" Puzhaty called after him.

Kobot dithered on the spot, then went over to him.

"Why're you running away from me like that?"

"I'm not, it's . . . I had to . . ."

"Don't give me that. I saw you coming towards the door."

It was already dark, which lent the scene a sinister undertone.

"Well I was, but then I decided to go to the shop!" Kobot said in a hysterical voice. Puzhaty said nothing. His face was in shadow and the pointy stars on his uniform buttons glittered. Kobot said nothing for a while to keep him company, then went off behind the building, where he hung about for half an hour to throw him off the scent.

* * *

That evening before he went to bed Kobot glanced briefly into the kitchen, then started back and froze behind the door. Puzhaty, all red and sweaty and clutching a glass in his hand, was whispering to Fyodor: "That Kobot, I reckon he's a bad lot. He had a shifty look about him this morning, twisting that ugly mug of his every which way, afraid of something, he is. Then I'm on my way down to the shop for some vermouth just now when I look, and there he fucking is – that bloody Kobot! Well, he spots me and he goes darting off, hiding behind his collar. Right, I thought, you're up to no good . . . Not only that, when I ask him where he works he tells me: 'At the Fuckanical!' Right, I thought, I've got your number!"

"At the Mechanical! I work at the Mechanical!" Kobot babbled from behind the door, forgetting the situation he was in.

The effect produced was sudden and powerful.

Even Fyodor glanced at the door in fright, but Puzhaty leapt to his feet and went dashing out of the kitchen, colliding with the wild-eyed Kobot. They stood there in silence for a while, almost pressed against each other, their eyes glittering, breathing agitatedly.

"Aha! . . ." said Puzhaty, adjusting his vest.

Kobot ran off to his room, swaying as he went.

"Morons! What kind of imbecility is this?" he muttered. "Ugh! It's all so . . . Ugh! Absolute imbecility."

He went over to the mirror and gazed into it intensely. The mirror's wise, matt glow framed a face distorted by despair. Incapable of doing anything else, Kobot went on standing in front of the mirror for a long time, twisting his head this way and that and baring his teeth. This senseless activity provided some kind of outlet for the tension that had overwhelmed him out of the blue.

The alarm clock ticked with steady menace.

The door opened without a knock and Puzhaty came into the room, already in his uniform and boots. Without asking permission, he sat down at the table, took out a cigarette and, as he softened it between his fingers, began surveying the modest but pleasantly arranged room.

Kobot stood there at the mirror like a thief caught with his hand in the till.

"Kobot, just what is it you're trying to hide?" Puzhaty said slowly.

"Alexei . . . Mr Puzhaty, I have absolutely no idea what . . . why you . . . are asking me that."

"Ah, so I'm the one who's to blame, am I? I'm harassing you? It's all my fault, is it? Is that what you're trying to say?"

"No, but you were telling Fyodor . . . Back there . . ."

"Go on, go on. I'm listening."

Kobot said nothing.

"Come on, I'm listening to you."

"You were saying I hide behind my collar . . ."

"Enough of this gibberish! But by the way, though, if you want to discuss that particular incident: after I met you I was in the shop. Do you still want to tell me that was where you were going?"

Kobot said nothing.

"You, Kobot, are clearly feeling worried about me moving into the flat, aren't you? Yes or no?"

The wine glasses in the sideboard gave a shrill shriek. The ticking of the clock was terrifying.

"Isn't it about time you stopped playing dumb?" Puzhaty roared, stubbing his cigarette out hard on the tabletop.

Kobot twitched as though he'd had an electric shock, then ran over to the window. Puzhaty stood up, knocking over his chair, and went out of the room.

Kobot gazed wide-eyed into empty space. When he came to, he dashed out into the corridor, put on his coat and ran out into the street.

* * *

Outside, everything seemed like a nightmare: long gusts of wind blowing out of every side-street, passers-by marching like soldiers from one bus-stop to the next, street lamps, cars . . . There was nowhere to hide.

It was late evening before Kobot could bring himself to go back home.

Leaving his coat on, he tiptoed through to his room and took his coat off there, made several rounds of the room and then stuck his head out into the corridor.

From the kitchen he could hear the violent clinking of glasses and Puzhaty's booming voice: "He's a hostile element, mark my words! As hostile as I've ever seen. And there's nothing I can do – I can see he's hostile all right, an enemy, but I can't nail him. But just you wait, he won't give me the slip, or my name's not Alexei Puzhaty! He can't escape, he'll give himself away!"

* * *

The next day Kobot chickened out and didn't go home at all. For the first time in a long, long time he spent the night somewhere else. He asked a friend, or rather, a colleague from work, to put him up, and he had a good enough time there, too – they played cards and talked about work, but it's always difficult staying in a strange place, and awkward too.

Afterwards they went to work together; somehow you can forget your troubles there, all the time you're not at work seems so short and insignificant. To unwind completely after work Kobot went to the cinema to see *Colonel Zorin's Story,* and set off back home completely calm. Just how long could he go on being frightened by that idiot of a militiaman anyway? He just had to make things clear to him, point out just how stupidly he was carrying on; it would be better still if he was really short with him, really put him in his place. No, to hell with him, he wasn't worth it!

Kobot went into the flat, took off his coat (he even brushed it), went through to his room without trying to hide, then sat down calmly at the table with the book *Notes on the History of the Present Time*.

Almost immediately Puzhaty came into the room and made himself comfortable facing Kobot. Kobot tore his eyes away from his book, gave Puzhaty a cold look, then immersed himself once again in his reading. The militiaman drummed his fingers on the table, staring sarcastically at Kobot as he read.

"Reading a book then, are we?"

Kobot kept his eyes fixed on the book.

"Right then, put that book down! Look at me!" Puzhaty yelled, more terrifyingly than ever before, slamming his open hand down hard on the tabletop. Everything creaked and rattled and the book fell to the floor.

Kobot was left without anything to fix his eyes on and he glanced in agony at Puzhaty. Puzhaty was sitting there all red and breathing heavily.

"Mr Puzhaty, I really think it's time . . ." Kobot began.

"Kobot, what were you up to last night?" Puzhaty said, interrupting him.

"Me . . . What? I was sleeping, staying with . . ."

"Where? What address?"

"But what . . . what's this . . . at work, that is, with a colleague . . ."

"Interesting work you have, I see . . . What's the address, I said?"

Kobot realised it would be best not to make any fuss but just answer the questions calmly, so Puzhaty could let off steam, realise he was wrong and leave him alone. But he actually couldn't recall his colleague's address just at that moment, not in this frantic state.

"I can't recall exactly just at present. I can show you where it is, or I can ask tomorrow."

"So we can't remember where we were last night? Or maybe we don't want to remember?"

The swollen veins in Puzhaty's neck glinted in the light. He stood up, took a careful look round the room and went out, slamming the door behind him.

Kobot groaned, jumped to his feet and began dashing backwards and forwards. He ran over to the door, but not all the way, so it wouldn't look as though he was eavesdropping, and froze. After a while he heard the doorbell ring – it was Pyotr, Maxim's pupil, who'd brought some vermouth. He danced about, humming some oriental tune. Fyodor pompously asserted that port was more pantheistic than vermouth. Suddenly Puzhaty's domineering voice rang out.

"Quiet! Take care when moving around the flat! Kobot's here!"

* * *

Late that evening, when everyone had quietened down, Kobot tiptoed along the corridor to the toilet, listening warily at every step. He felt for the door, opened it slowly so that it wouldn't squeak, went inside and began closing it ever so gently.

There was a sudden crash and the light went on in the corridor.

Puzhaty grabbed hold of the door that was almost closed and heaved it towards himself with a strident yell: "Stop right there, you swine! Now there's no escape!"

Kobot clutched at the handle till his hands bled, but the door continued to open implacably. Kobot screeched like a cornered animal and covered his head with his hands.

Puzhaty stood there for about half a minute, looming in the doorway like a stone statue, and then without saying a word he strode off to his own room, leaving a disturbing trail of stale wine fumes in his wake.

* * *

Three hours or so later, when Kobot was just beginning to nod off on the sofa where he'd stretched out without bothering to undress, there was a sudden, loud clatter of boot heels in the corridor. There was a terrible crackling noise right in his ears, and then a voice speaking through a megaphone.

"Attention, Kobot! You are surrounded! All resistance is futile!

Come out and give yourself up!"

Kobot rubbed his eyes till they hurt and sank his teeth into the flesh of his arm.

"I repeat, Kobot, all resistance is futile! Come out and give yourself up!"

And then that tense crackling of anticipation again.

A door slammed, then he heard Maxim's voice.

"I'll teach you to go yelling the place down, you bastard! We already had one shit yelling his head off in the middle of the night, and now we've got another!"

"Everyone remain in their rooms!" Puzhaty answered through the megaphone.

"I'll give you rooms, you asshole!"

For a while the footsteps in the corridor continued, with the lights being switched on and off – Kobot was almost in a faint. He ripped open the front of his shirt and lay down on his back, breathing hoarsely.

* * *

When morning was already near Kobot sank into a painful, restless sleep. He woke frequently, instantly forgetting his nightmare visions, for reality seemed even worse, more vile and incomprehensible. He woke up at the slightest rustle, stretching out his neck and peering sleepily around in all directions.

When it began to grow brighter in the room and the vague masses of the furniture began to assume the contours of forms that were not yet clear, the door burst open and he heard Puzhaty's voice speaking from the doorway: "Stay where you are! Move a muscle and I shoot! Hands up!"

A black figure lunged out of the darkness and made a dash for the light-switch.

Kobot bounced upright like a spring, removing the safety catch and pressing the trigger in a single movement.

A shot roared out and the black figure slumped to the floor.

* * *

People began bustling about in the corridor. Maxim switched on the light. They turned Puzhaty over on to his back. There was a gruesome patch of blood spreading across his blue uniform, right over his heart. Kobot cringed into the corner of the sofa, constantly examining his hands and groping underneath himself.

Everyone stared in stupefaction at the bulky, incongruous corpse.

EPILOGUE

Puzhaty's incomprehensible death astounded all the inhabitants of the flat. Kobot pestered Maxim and Fyodor for days, asking whether they believed it wasn't him who killed Puzhaty. They wanted to believe him, although they couldn't see how it could be anyone else. But then it couldn't have been Kobot, who'd never held a gun in his life, and anyway . . .

They didn't take Kobot away; it wasn't clear why, they just didn't take him. They hushed everything up. Maxim's pupil Pyotr seemed to think that they were all pulling his leg – he called Kobot "our Rinaldo Rinaldini" and composed a poem about him:

With his iron fetters jangling,
By armed guards is Kobot led.
Still unwashed, one early morning
He did shoot his neighbour dead . . .
Now his old, free life recalling,
He limps onward, cursing fate,
With his iron fetters rattling,
Weeping now it is too late.

Pyotr didn't enjoy his joke for long.

When he heard the poem, Maxim gave him a smack on the head and said: "D'you want to wind up dead too, asshole?"

VISITORS
(a conversation)

The room of Pyotr, Maxim's pupil. A large table, a bookcase full of books – pretty good books, but desperately tatty, and many of them bearing library stamps. A half-dismantled tape-deck. All sorts of stuff. Lying under the bed instead of one of its legs is a pile of magazines and books, while the leg itself is lying right there beside it. The room is relatively clean; there are three bottles of port and some bread on the table – Pyotr is clearly expecting visitors.

Pyotr is sitting at the table with a book. He looks at the clock, then takes a bottle from the table, opens it, pours out half a glass and drinks it slowly. The doorbell rings.

Pyotr quickly finishes his drink, pours himself another one the same size and drinks that down too, clearly to bolster his courage. We hear the front door of the apartment being opened.

PYOTR *(clearing his throat and shouting)*: That's for me!

He runs out of the room and comes back with his visitors. They are Fyodor's pupil Vasilii; Alexei Zhitoi, a tough-looking type; Motin, an artist yet to make a name for himself; Vovik, who is weak all over except in his jaws, which constant shame-faced clenching have made strong; Samoilov.

ZHITOI: Look, he's started already! Okay, guys, we'll have to catch up. *(He takes two bottles of port out of his briefcase – a cheaper brand than the one on the table.)*
VASILII: Hang on, let's make some snacks first. I haven't had a bite all day.
ZHITOI: Agh, I just hate it when people start fussing about and running around. Vovik, have you got any sausage?

Vovik extracts some sausage and two bottles of vermouth – naturally, not Italian – out of a bag bearing the inscription "Demis Roussos".

PYOTR: Why in hell's name do you go buying vermouth when there's port in the shop?
VOVIK: I didn't have enough for two bottles of port.
PYOTR: I almost destroyed my stomach with that gut-rot.

Pyotr serves out the salami and the bread and brings in some boiled potatoes from the kitchen. Everybody sits down except Samoilov, who stands there with his hands in his pockets and stares at the centre of the table with an ironical expression. Everybody drinks and eats with the words "okay then" and "off we go"; Samoilov twirls a large glass in his fingers, scrutinising it derisively.

VASILII: Sit down. Why're you just standing there like the Bronze Horseman?

Samoilov sits down and smiles condescendingly.

ZHITOI: Let's all have another straight off to get us in the mood.

He pours. Almost everybody drinks up. Vasilii gulps his wine down in one, the way Fyodor usually does. By contrast, Pyotr takes a mouthful and sets his glass down, then takes another mouthful, like Maxim.

VASILII *(to Motin)*: What's up with you? Let go, will you? Relax.
MOTIN: Aw, bugger it . . . When I get off work I'm no bloody good for anything. And they wonder why we drink . . . We don't drink anything like enough!
ZHITOI: That's right! *(He pours everybody another glass.)*
VASILII: The fact that we drink is an expression of our despairing philosophical frenzy.
SAMOILOV: We drink because when we're drunk the hangover's not so painful.
MOTIN: I'm absolutely knackered after doing that job. Trying to

paint pictures is just a waste of time. I haven't done anything for a year now. If I do pick up the brush, I can't bring myself to squeeze out the paint, I feel so miserable – what can I paint in an hour when I'm already knackered?

VOVIK: What about Sundays, then?

MOTIN (*extremely annoyed*): I have to recover my bloody strength on Sundays! I've got a whole week of hard grafting to get through! And what about clearing up the flat? And when am I supposed to take my son out? Or go to the shop?

PYOTR: Everyone lives the way that he has . . .

MOTIN (*interrupting*): Andrei Bely says somewhere that even though they weren't friends, Blok sent him a thousand roubles so he could spend six months studying anthroposophy without worrying about money. Anthroposophy, ah? Those bastards had it made! (*He downs his drink in one.*) Release me from this hard labour for six months and I'll show you some anthroposophy! . . .

ZHITOI: But those guys of yours . . . what's their names . . . Maxim and Fyodor – they don't work, do they, Pyotr?

PYOTR: No, they don't.

MOTIN (*spitefully*): So how come?

PYOTR: They manage it somehow or other.

VOVIK: How long since they've worked?

PYOTR: I don't actually know . . . Vasilii, do you know?

Vasilii shakes his head.

SAMOILOV: But what do they do?

MOTIN: Not a thing! They drink! Why the hell you waste your time on them I don't know. A right pair of winos.

ZHITOI: Never mind all that, let's have a drink! (*He pours.*)

MOTIN: What kind of sausage is this?

VOVIK: "Doctor's".

VASILII: No, with Maxim and Fyodor it's not that simple . . .

MOTIN (*interrupting*): Come off it . . . I've seen your Maxim and Fyodor, and that's enough for me. Gen-u-wine alconauts.

ZHITOI: Hey, listen, didn't I hear someone got killed round at their place?

At that moment Samoilov switches on the tape deck. It plays a poor-quality recording of Ellington's "Caravan".

MOTIN: Shut that thing up!
SAMOILOV: Why don't we put something else on? Pyotr, have you got any Beatles?
PYOTR: No, not right now. Leave that on, just turn it down.
SAMOILOV: And what is it?
ZHITOI *(to Vovik)*: Will you drink up, for God's sake? Can't you see we're all waiting for you!
PYOTR: Ellington.
ZHITOI: Right, I'm opening the vermouth. What d'you reckon?
VASILII: Yeah, go on.
SAMOILOV: No, I don't want Ellington.
VASILII: I say leave him on!

Zhitoi pours.

VOVIK: So who was it got killed?
PYOTR *(with a glance at Vasilii)*: One of Maxim and Fyodor's neighbours in the flat, a militiaman. He got killed.
ZHITOI: Who did it?
PYOTR: No one knows.
ZHITOI: What? Didn't they find them? Where was he killed?
PYOTR *(reluctantly)*: Right there, in the flat.
ZHITOI: There's a turn-up! Who else lives in the flat?
PYOTR: One other guy . . . called Kobot.
ZHITOI: So maybe he killed him? Where in the flat was this militiaman killed? What with?
PYOTR: He was shot . . . In that guy Kobot's room.
ZHITOI: Did they take Kobot in, then?
PYOTR: No.

ZHITOI: We ought to drink to that. *(He pours.)*

VASILII: No, no, the story's not that simple. Pyotr and me didn't know the militiaman, I just saw him in the kitchen a couple of times but, you know, it was obvious he was the kind of man who thought he had the right to judge other people. People like that are the devil's best bait – if he doesn't kill someone, then he'll get killed himself, sooner or later, so you have to be prepared in advance . . . like a natural disaster. That is, it wasn't like he just simply turned up . . .

SAMOILOV: Who killed him, though?

VASILII: That's the problem. Seems like it was Kobot, only not really him. For a while Kobot was completely under the control of the powers of evil. He became a perfect channel for them.

ZHITOI: I don't get you.

VASILII: Well, what happened was the militiaman suspected Kobot of something – he kept on and on hassling him . . .

ZHITOI: And so Kobot naturally . . .

VASILII: No. How can I explain it . . . it's like if every day you tell someone he's a pig, then he'll actually turn into a pig. He'll just start believing it himself. Lamaism has this teaching that says the world is not reality, but the totality of ideas about the world, that is, if everybody closes their eyes and thinks of the sky as red instead of blue, then it really will turn red.

Samoilov glances round the room ironically, raising a quizzical eyebrow. Zhitoi is clearly struggling.

MOTIN: Listen, maybe that's enough, okay?

VASILII: Just a moment. You see Puzhaty was so certain Kobot was a criminal, he just wore him down, till Kobot got completely confused and started believing it himself.

ZHITOI: And bumped him off?

VASILII: No he didn't! Not exactly . . . Puzhaty just invented a demon. He created it and it killed him.

SAMOILOV: *There was a priest who had a dog*
                And really, really loved it.

> *The doggy ate a piece of meat.*
> *And so he went and killed it.*

Vasilii shrugs hopelessly. He drinks.

VOVIK: Is that Ellington too?

Pyotr nods.

VASILII: Kobot didn't kill anyone! He could easily have been sound asleep at the time; but every evil thought is a demon that . . .
PYOTR *(interrupting)*: That's not the point, Vasilii. At first I just didn't believe Puzhaty had been killed, let alone that Kobot had killed him. I even wrote a little poem . . .
VASILII: So?
PYOTR: Maxim said to me – I remember his very words – "D'you want to wind up dead too?"
ZHITOI: But in the meantime, let's have a drink! *(He pours.)*
PYOTR: D'you understand what he meant by that? That a man like Kobot, a genuinely simple individual, a man with no distinguishing features, a philistine – that a man like that is best left alone, it's best not to mess with a man like that, you never know what resources a man like that has. It's people like that, the ones you don't even notice, who control your fate – Motin, weren't you complaining about that?
MOTIN: Come on, that's enough of this . . .
PYOTR: That's what Maxim said, leave him alone, or you'll wind up dead.
SAMOILOV: I don't understand why you keep quoting this Maxim like he was your teacher.
MOTIN: Like little kids, Pyotr and Vasilii, the pair of them! Little kids with a new toy, them and their winos . . .
PYOTR: But they really have given us . . . taught us something . . .
SAMOILOV: What?
PYOTR: It's hard to say in concrete terms. You've read about Zen, haven't you?

MOTIN: I know about it. I was the one who gave you *An Introduction to Zen Buddhism*!

PYOTR: Well, don't you think Maxim and Fyodor often behave as though . . .

MOTIN: According to Zen?

Everybody laughs, even those who have never heard of Zen Buddhism. Vasilii smiles.

PYOTR: What's wrong?

ZHITOI: What's wrong is, we need another drink! *(He pours.)*

MOTIN *(to Samoilov)*: Turn it up. Or is that Ellington too?

PYOTR: No, hang on, don't turn it up. I'll tell you something that happened. Lying outside the house where Maxim and Fyodor live there's this huge tree stump – a great round thing it is – and every time Fyodor walks past it he says: "Just look at that chunk!" So one time I said to him: "Why do you keep saying that? I already know it's a chunk." And then Maxim – he was walking along with us – shows me his fist and says: "You ever seen that?"

Everybody laughs.

MOTIN: Is that it?

PYOTR: Yes.

General laughter.

MOTIN *(spreading his arms wide, with a deferential grimace)*: Definitely not for those with weak nerves . . .

PYOTR: What's there to laugh at?

The laughter, which was about to die away, grows louder.

PYOTR: Aagh! . . .

ZHITOI: Right, what I say is: stay dry for a year, but not to drink right now would be a sin! *(He pours.)*

PYOTR: So what do you think Maxim meant by that phrase? Stop laughing and hear me out! He meant that although I might, for instance, have seen Maxim's fist plenty of times, it could manifest itself in a quite different capacity, and it does, every time it manifests itself. In the same way every object in the world, every phenomenon, no matter how ordinary it might be, should command our unfailing attention; for everything can change, everything does change – but we're the prisoners of dogmatism. It was this paying attention to everything that Fyodor was expressing, apparently so obsessively, by drawing attention to the chunk of wood. He was apprehending it over and over again.

A pause.

SAMOILOV: That's what I call a shaggy dog story.

VOVIK: No, it's all very interesting, of course, but Maxim can't really have meant that when he showed you his fist.

VASILII: To each his own. That is, everyone understands according to his ability.

MOTIN *(angrily)*: Hey now, watch it!

PYOTR: Yes, but that's not the point. What do you mean by "he didn't mean it"? Of course, Maxim and Fyodor do everything intuitively . . .

MOTIN: For goodness' sake! No more!

VOVIK: No, let him finish what he's saying!

PYOTR: . . . But even so, they understand what they're doing too. Here's another example. One day I noticed that when Fyodor got to the front of the queue at the kiosk he didn't buy any beer, he just walked away.

ZHITOI *(astonished)*: Why?

PYOTR: That's what I asked: why? Especially since afterwards Fyodor joins the end of the queue again. And then Fyodor told me: "If a created work is to dwell in eternity it should not be taken to its conclusion."

The others smirk and chortle.

SAMOILOV: That's just plain lunacy.

ZHITOI: Somehow I don't quite get it. Let's have a drink! *(He pours.)*

PYOTR: Well, the phrase itself, "If a created work is to dwell in eternity it should not be taken to its conclusion", was something I said to him once. It's a well-known principle in the Orient. In China, for instance, even when they built the Emperor's palace, they always used to leave one corner unfinished. Same thing here. To be quite honest, Fyodor's not all that bright, he's not really a very big man – so where can he apply that principle? Only like that, on that level. He's stating that high principles are needed even in the small things. That's the most difficult thing of all . . . Of course, in this instance it appears comical, but that makes it all the more obvious. You could say he applied the principle in completely the wrong way – it's one thing not to finish creating something, to break off somewhere close to perfection, but quite another not even to begin, to halt at the preliminary stage of standing in a queue. But that's just him being ironical with me, saying it's not always right to grasp at every principle that comes your way.

And he also did it to see what the reaction would be from asses like you, who don't know how to do anything but bray.

SAMOILOV: Drop it, drop it, will you? No need to get angry.

MOTIN: What's the bloody point in wasting the evening on this pretentious shite? Enough already!

VOVIK: Oh, come on . . . Okay . . .

ZHITOI: Just drop it, guys! Vovik, are you ever going to drink up?

VASILII: Vovik, I reckon you've had enough.

MOTIN: Hey, Samoilov! The tape finished ages ago! Put the other side on.

SAMOILOV: What's on it?

PYOTR: Ellington.

SAMOILOV: Haven't you got anything else?

VASILII: Ah, put Ellington on, sod him! *(To Motin)* So, how's the job going?

MOTIN: Ah, bugger off, and take the job with you.

VOVIK: No, but it's interesting what that Fyodor . . .

ZHITOI: Pyotr! Where d'you put your glass? Give it here, it's over by the tape-deck.

Samoilov turns the tape over and turns up the volume. Everybody has to raise his voice to speak.

PYOTR *(as though talking to himself)*: You fail to understand one simple thing. Shestov put it very well: mankind has become insanely obsessed by the idea of rational understanding. Take Maxim and Fyodor: . . . just between you and me, they're pretty stupid . . .

MOTIN *(sarcastically)*: You don't say!

PYOTR: . . . and certainly not any less ordinary than we are. But strange as it may seem, they've managed to escape from this intolerably commonplace, ordinary world . . . slipped out the back way, if you like. And so . . .

VASILII: Pyotr, just shut up before it's too late.

SAMOILOV: Vovik, pass over the sausage, if there's any left.

ZHITOI: Great sausage today. Something about it, I just can't get enough!

VASILII: You may be a lotus-eater, Pyotr, but you're the one who's obsessed with the idea of rational understanding. Zen Buddhism's not much cop if you can chew it to death like that.

PYOTR: Then you try explaining about Maxim!

VASILII: You're obviously just drunk. Maxim and Fyodor are secret heroes, you can't explain them.

ZHITOI: Bloody hell! We haven't finished the port yet! Vasilii, you've still got another bottle!

VASILII: That's right! You get it. It's in that plastic bag over there!

SAMOILOV: Pyotr, where can I put Vovik?

PYOTR: There's a sleeping-bag over there under the bed. Put him under the window.

MOTIN: No wonder he switched off, the way you've been wanking on about those slobs Maxim and Fyodor. It's amazing we haven't all

switched off. If only you could tell it so it made sense, instead of all these tankas and koans. And what's "Monogatari", anyway?
ZHITOI: Hey, guys! Let's just settle down to a quiet little drink! *(He pours.)*
SAMOILOV: Hey, quiet! Is that McCartney?
PYOTR: Yeah, sounds like it.
SAMOILOV: Quiet! Let's listen.

They listen to the end of the tape, tapping their feet. Samoilov sings along.

MOTIN: Let's have something else . . . Have you got any Tanya Ivanova?
PYOTR: No.
ZHITOI: Shame! Great music for drinking to, I tell you . . .
VASILII: She only goes with vodka.
PYOTR: So what time is it? Damn and blast, it's after nine! Okay. The port's all gone anyway – we'll all have to chip in and try the restaurant!

Everybody except the sleeping Vovik and Samoilov take out all the money they have left. Zhitoi dashes off to the restaurant. Motin puts a new tape on, at random.

MOTIN: What's that?
PYOTR: Ellington.
MOTIN: Did you lay in a stock for winter or something?

A pause. They have to listen to Ellington for a while as they wait for Zhitoi. Everyone seems good-natured and relaxed.

VASILII *(to Motin)*: Painted anything recently?
MOTIN: Not really . . . I've no time . . .
VASILII: Who has? No point just waiting, though. Blok's not going to come up with another thousand.

MOTIN *(seriously)*: I'm waiting for my son to grow up.
VASILII: Ah . . . How old is he now?
MOTIN: About two.
VASILII: About two! You mean you don't know exactly?
MOTIN: About two! And I'm not really waiting for anything!
VASILII: That's not possible. Any atheist has to be waiting for something. We're all waiting for this damn rotten present to come to an end and a new one to begin. When we were in school we were waiting to graduate. At college we were waiting too, dreaming of qualifying as soon as possible. Now we're waiting for our son to grow up, or even better, for when we retire. Even the happiest of us keep on hurrying the future along. Isn't that terrible? Quick, quick, get through this as quickly as we can, then get through something else, and after that . . . what do you reckon – death?

Like a swimmer swimming with all his might, swimming as fast as he can, paying no attention to anything else, just swimming towards his goal. When he knows perfectly well he's swimming towards a waterfall. And then someone suggests to the swimmer that he ought to be an optimist.
PYOTR: Not thinking about death saves you.
VASILII: Saves you from what? Then insanity's even better. Here we go talking in circles again! I've heard it before: "life is an end in itself", "there's no way you can improve on the wisdom of life". What are you all waiting for?
PYOTR: I wonder what's taking Zhitoi so long?
MOTIN: God almighty! I'm so sick of it all!

A pause. Motin falls into a doze.

PYOTR: Go Si wrote: "In those days when my father would take up the brush, he would always sit without fail at a clean desk by a bright window, light the incense, take his best brush and excellent ink, wash his hands and clean his inkwell. It was as though he were receiving a great guest. His spirit was pure, his thoughts were focused. Then he would begin working."

Or take a Renaissance artist – he would fast for two days, and only after saying lengthy prayers, then banishing everyone from the house and waiting for the dust to settle, would he take up his brush.

That's the only way that'll do for Motin too.

But as a matter of fact, it was Maxim who told me about Go Si. And guess where it was – in that shitty little room of theirs, holding a glass that had never been washed, full of the same gut-rot we're drinking now. Why did they need to keep things so pure in olden times? So they wouldn't be distracted by the outside world. But maybe we've attained a state of realisation that the external is also important? I just remembered something Akhmatova says: "If you but knew from what filth poems grow, knowing no shame . . ."

Vasilii laughs, unable to restrain himself.

PYOTR: What's up?
VASILII: He's attained a state! *(Laughs.)*
PYOTR: What's wrong with that?
VASILII: Nothing. Everything you say's right, Pyotr, let me give you a kiss. You're a Faustian man, Pyotr. Faustian. Now what was it I wanted to say about Faust? . . . Yes! So Maxim told you about Go Si?
PYOTR: What of it?
VASILII: And how did he know? Where did he find out?
PYOTR: He just knows, that's all.

A pause.

SAMOILOV: Pyotr, okay if I lie on the bed till Zhitoi gets back?
PYOTR: Go ahead.
VASILII *(suddenly drunk)*: Pyotr, would you like me to tell you who killed Puzhaty?
PYOTR: It wasn't you, was it?
VASILII: Me? Naah, not me. Maxim killed him.
PYOTR *(laughing)*: And I suppose it was you, brother Karamazov, who taught him how to kill?

VASILII: So why didn't they take Kobot in? It was perfectly obvious they should have. Why?

PYOTR: Well, why?

VASILII: You mean you haven't noticed anything strange about Maxim? I noticed it at the very beginning, when Kobot had just moved in. He came in once to say something about cleaning the flat, wanted to put up a schedule of who should wash the floor when, and then he asked Maxim: "And where do you work?" I could see Maxim was annoyed, and he said to him: "Where do you work?"; "At the Mechanical"; "Then you should have stayed in your bloody Mechanical!"

PYOTR: Well, it was the right answer.

VASILII: Sure it was right, from a Zen viewpoint, but I thought, really though, where does he work, if he has money for drinking every day?

PYOTR: Oh, not that again! And what's Kobot got to do with anything?

VASILII: Kobot's got nothing to do with anything, but how could Maxim and Fyodor go to Japan? Or what about this – how old is Fyodor? Forty at most. Well, let's say he was born before the war, even back in the twenties. How could he have had connections with underground activists before the revolution?

PYOTR: Vasilii, what are you on about? You mean you take everything literally?

VASILII: Okay then, let's say . . . that's okay . . . but they were definitely in Japan. Don't interrupt me now, I've got to work this out for myself.

Right, so . . . just a moment . . . no, now I've got it . . . I've guessed it . . . what happened to Maxim is a manifest form of what happens to many of us without even being noticed. Maxim sold his soul to the devil.

I don't know when or why, most likely it was done on a sudden whim, like all the important things in our lives – wham! bam! – then let's see what happens. So what happens? He drank yesterday, and he drinks the same way today.

PYOTR: But how, why . . .?

VASILII: Shut it, will you! I asked you not to interrupt. Maybe he just didn't have a clue what he was getting and what he was giving for it. He just woke up one morning and there was the devil waiting for instructions: "So what can I do for you, Maxim?"; "I can't seem to think of anything much. No, I fancy a smoke"; "There you go, then, light up. Fancy a beer?"; "You mean you can get me beer too? Off you go then". Maybe that was how Maxim bartered away his soul, for a ciggy and a mug of beer. You know, some very clever people sell their souls just for some clever turn of phrase.

Well, of course, the devil's not satisfied with that, that way there was no deal done. True evil and the loss of the soul come when the devil can act through a man. Get it? The actual contract itself is a load of nonsense. What's important are the deeds a man performs as a consequence of that contract, get it? The devil's quite willing to lend a hand even without any contract. All he wants is to lend a hand – and the man's lost his soul anyway.

PYOTR: Evil is the punishment of oneself.

MOTIN *(raising his head from the table)*: Everything in this world is so much filth, shit and puke, only painting's eternal. *(Lowers his head on to the table.)*

VASILII: Eh? Right. So, what the devil needs to do is give Maxim some idea of the path of evil.

PYOTR: That's all very fine, but how, why?

ZHITOI *(appearing in the doorway, singing)*: Because it's vodka. How hard it is to get that first glass down!

Pyotr and Vasilii leap to their feet with cries of greeting. Samoilov gets up from the bed with a warm smile.

SAMOILOV *(with feeling)*: Aah, guys!

PYOTR: Did you just buy one?

ZHITOI: One vodka and another vermouth!

Pyotr, Vasilii and Zhitoi take each other by the hand and dance, shrieking and bellowing excitedly. The tape-deck is playing

Ellington's piano piece "Through the Glass".

ZHITOI: Hey, Motin, enough dozing, get up!
MOTIN *(without raising his head)*: I'm okay . . . all right, just a moment, just let me keep my head down for a while . . .
ZHITOI *(in a tone of warm benediction)*: Right guys, okay, I'm pouring. *(He pours.)* All paid for and poured out!

Everybody except Motin drinks, with the words "that hit the spot", "great stuff", and "give me some water".

SAMOILOV: Pyotr, why haven't you got any women?
PYOTR: What d'you mean? Where?
SAMOILOV: Well, here we are drinking, and we were drinking earlier, but there's not a single woman to be seen.
PYOTR *(dolefully)*: Stop it. Because . . .
ZHITOI: Pity. It's more fun with women. But then, sod them, all the more for us. *(He pours.)* You know, Ellington's not that bad after all.
SAMOILOV: Have you got a guitar?
PYOTR: No! No!
SAMOILOV: Pity . . . Have the neighbours got one?
PYOTR: No.
ZHITOI: Okay, guys, we've supped some good stuff today. Another bottle each and we could look folks straight in the eye tomorrow.
SAMOILOV: Shall we go and get a guitar?
ZHITOI: Where from?
SAMOILOV: My young lad's got a friend round here. Maybe he's got one.
ZHITOI: Are you crazy? If we go, they'll polish everything off!
VASILII: What do you want a guitar for?
SAMOILOV: Come on, Lyoshka, let's make a dash for it, it's not far.
ZHITOI: Ha! Screw you, then! Let's have one for the road! *(He drinks.)* Make sure you don't overdo it while we're gone!
PYOTR: Samoilov's behaving himself today, no flash stuff.
VASILII: Yeah, we ought to set up a monument.

PYOTR: Tell me, what was that yarn you were spinning about Maxim? That he sold his soul to the devil? Were you trying to tell some kind of parable or are you just pissed?

VASILII: Why pissed? Ah . . . right, I was just saying that what the devil needs to do is give Maxim some concept of evil. Shouldn't be too hard, the world's full of evil, and here's Maxim with the devil to help him out.

PYOTR: He always helps everyone out.

VASILII: Well, anyway, the devil eggs Maxim on – why not take the opportunity? Go on, expand your horizons; if you like I can give you the knowledge of all books, if you like we can go travelling so you can learn everything from experience. After all, to start with the devil needs to make Maxim a bit smarter, so he can find things to tempt him with; and in the second place, as Metropolitan Antonii says, there's no law for the beasts, and He doesn't call them to account. But those that do know are held to account according to their knowledge. Ignorance of the law exempts you from responsibility.

PYOTR: I don't think so. The wheel of samsa . . .

VASILII: Don't interrupt me, please. I've had your wheel of samsara up to here. Of course, it's not exactly like that. But you can't really imagine a man turning away from God for a mug of beer, can you? And basically Maxim really doesn't want anything, no matter how deep you dig – no treasure or power or seductive succubi. He's as pure as a Greek cynic, and he knows that he knows nothing, and as for his drinking – that means nothing . . . So he says, I suppose I could do a spot of travelling. Maxim and the devil set off on their journey. Way off to the other end of the world, and they saw . . . they saw real live Red Indians, living all year round in tourist tents and never working. And they were in Mainz, where the Main falls into the Rhine; they saw a fire and a man who jumped out of a window into a bed-sheet. They were in Holstinia, they were in Pannonia, but they didn't see anything special. They were in Ireland, they saw a man with a beard and tits down to his belly-button. In Amsterdam they saw a shop with eighty different types of bottled beer, not counting the cans. They were in Savatthi and Djettavan and they saw the power station destroyed. They were in Morocco, where almost everyone's an Arab and some of them are wrapped up in bed-sheets. They were in the Sandwich Islands, they saw a green fish that makes you puke just to look at it. They were in Orekhovo-Zuevo, where there's a long queue for the beer kiosk. One guy who didn't want to lose his place kept pissing right there in the queue. Out of all his travels Maxim liked this guy most of all, and they decided to take him with them. He was Fyodor.

PYOTR: Ah! I thought you were going to wind up saying Fyodor and Mephistopheles were the same person.

VASILII: After that they were in Ionian Prien, they saw the monument to Biant with the inscription "Born in the glorious fields of Prien, he rests beneath this slab, the torchbearer of the Ionians – Biant". Of course, the inscription was in Ancient Greek and Maxim couldn't read it. And that was the first time he regretted not being clever. They were in Thebes, they saw a wise man there and when they asked him what he'd learned from philosophy, he answered: "To chew beans and know no care." Maxim didn't understand, and again he wanted to be clever.

So he said to the devil: I want to be clever. Which was just what the devil wanted. Zap – and Maxim was as clever as . . . two Platos. Maxim sat there ever so clever without saying a word. He opened his mouth to say something, then he closed it again.

Pyotr pours impatiently.

VASILII: And now his intelligence was so great that he could understand his own inadequacy. After all, what good is naked intelligence? Except for becoming a philosopher, or a mathematician, or the leader of a nation. So what?

PYOTR: What d'you mean, so what?

VASILII: Wasn't it you who said everybody's obsessed with the self-evidentness of reason?

PYOTR *(irritated)*: I see where you're heading . . . If only you weren't drunk, you Westerniser, you'd have remembered that was how Mephistopheles tempted Faust:

> *Merely despise your mind and learning's light.*
> *All higher things that lend to man his might . . .*
> *And you are mine without another word!*

VASILII: Let me tell you about something that happened when I was at this conference on Dostoevsky. Everything was fine and cosy, all the speakers were pupils of Lotman or Bakhtin. Then the presentations came to an end and the discussions began . . . This old man walked out front, so nervous he was literally shaking. He hadn't prepared a speech, he didn't have any idea how to speak "like a book"; he just loved Dostoevsky. This old man was really happy and excited to have heard all those wise speeches and he wanted to thank all these wise men in the best way he knew how, but he spoke clumsily, because he was so excited. And then all these wise people who all knew Dostoevsky off by heart (think about it – Dostoevsky!) began laughing at him. As if to say, what do you mean sticking your piggy snout into our nice clean kitchen? Eh? So much for their intelligence. What d'you think Dostoevsky would have said to that?

Pyotr pours the drinks.

VASILII: These conference delegates are all very smart, so clever it's frightening! But intelligence alone isn't enough, is it?

Right then, so Maxim could feel that too. Hey, watch out, you've poured vermouth in my vodka! So what could Maxim do? What else could he ask for? He squeaked out in despair, he might as well go for it, if the way of God was closed to him – make me the Antichrist. But the devil says: Oh no, there's too many of you want that – but secretly he's delighted, thinks it's in the bag.

Then Maxim began to come to his senses, shook his head and

gathered his wits, only not completely. In that case, he said, I want the grace of God.

The devil just gaped at that one. Maxim gathered the rest of his wits, felt a pang of conscience and gave a bitter smile. How could he wrestle with the devil? God would forgive him . . .

ZHITOI *(entering the room)*: They've opened the vermouth already! Come on then, Samoilov!

Zhitoi pours. Samoilov makes a wise face as he tunes the guitar.

PYOTR: Pour some for us too.

ZHITOI: You'll get yours, don't piss yourself! *(He pours.)* Motin, are you going to sleep the entire night away?

VASILII: Let him sleep, his job really is bloody awful.

PYOTR *(to Vasilii)*: So how did it all end?

VASILII *(after a pause)*: Ah, right . . . I've lost the thread now. Well, Maxim won, which means he was left without any intelligence and they had to make their own way back from Japan.

ZHITOI: Who won?

VASILII: Never mind, I just . . .

PYOTR *(in a strict voice)*: What's all this got to do with Kobot? And working?

VASILII: Nothing at all, cool it.

PYOTR: Remember what Maxim said? D'you want to wind up dead too? And you go rambling on endlessly about the devil . . . Maxim's the last person that kind of fairy-tale fits. You're drunk already, I can see!

ZHITOI: Ah, we've supped some good stuff!

Samoilov plays snatches of various tunes with an intense expression on his face. He plays very quickly, swaying gently to the rhythm.

SAMOILOV *(slapping himself on the knee)*: Hey, Lyoshka, pour the drinks, let's get moving!

ZHITOI: Hey! Right! Let's go! *(He pours.)*

SAMOILOV: Okay, you start anything you like, and I'll join in. I love a good song.

A short pause.

VASILII: *The hubbub faded. I went out on stage,*
                  And there I leaned against the upright doorway,
                  Discerning in an echo far away
                  What was to happen in this day and age.

SAMOILOV *(joining in)*:
                  And at that time
                  Three pitchers were there standing there,
                  One filled with cocktail of carbolic,
                  One filled with extract of boot-polish,
                  And one filled to the very top with air!

Confusion and laughter.

ZHITOI: *From the island to the channel*
                  Of the river broad and deep
                  Sail the brightly-coloured vessels
                  Of bold Stenka Razin's fleet

SAMOILOV AND ZHITOI *(together)*:
                  And at that time
                  Three pitchers were there standing there,
                  One filled with cocktail of carbolic,
                  One filled with extract of boot-polish,
                  And one filled to the very top with air!

General laughter.

PYOTR *(with a dirty laugh)*:
                  And having trod the path of life halfway,

I found myself amidst a sombre forest,
Strayed from the path into the valley's deepest
              shade.

ALL *(together, exultantly)*:
              And at that time
              Three pitchers were there standing there,
              One filled with cocktail of carbolic,
              One filled with extract of boot-polish,
              And one filled to the very top with air!

LET'S GO TO TSARSKOE SELO!

One evening as he clutched a glass of beer Vasilii said: "Every single time I've been in Pushkin, they've always had crayfish in the bar."

"What price were they?" asked Pyotr.

"Eleven kopecks each."

"Big ones?"

"Naah, pretty small really . . . but that's not the point – have you ever seen them selling crayfish in a bar?"

"Yeah," said Pyotr, on a point of honour.

"Just where is this Pushkin?" asked Fyodor, twisting the cap off a bottle with his thumbnail.

"What d'you mean? Haven't you ever been there? Just outside Leningrad, twenty minutes on the local train."

" Shall we go, then?" Fyodor enquired in the direction of Maxim, who was slumped in an armchair like Menshikov in that picture by Surikov. Maxim didn't say anything.

"When? Right now, you mean?" asked Pyotr.

"Well when, then?"

"You have to go early in the morning, at the weekend; you can take a walk in the park there."

"Why don't you all bugger off with your Pushkin," Maxim interrupted. "Like little kids, never seen crayfish before . . ."

He got up and finished off his beer standing, then went over to the folding bed, took off his boots and lay down. The sound was a bit like two detachments of hussars crossing swords.

"Why shouldn't we go?" said Fyodor.

"What's the bloody point of dragging ourselves all that way. . .?" Maxim explained after a long pause, when no one was expecting an answer any longer.

Yes, of course, it's not easy to imagine Maxim and Fyodor anywhere outside the house and its surroundings, but just remember – they were in Japan, weren't they? . . .

"Why don't we go on Saturday?" Fyodor persisted.

"Go fuck yourself for all I care, night-feeder," said Maxim.

"Why 'night-feeder'?" Pyotr asked in surprise.

"Because whenever you get up at night for a piss, he's sitting in the kitchen naked, guzzling something out of a saucepan."

Everyone burst into laughter and Fyodor said with real feeling: "It's for the hangover! Of course, for the hangover, that is! And Kobot's always got soup on the go in his saucepan!"

They poured beer for everyone.

"Pyotr, give me a bottle, will you?" shouted Maxim, lying with his face to the wall.

Pyotr handed him a bottle of beer. Wheezing as though he were sick, Maxim turned round and started drinking it.

"Okay," he said, wiping the foam from his lips. "Today's Monday, right? We'll go on Saturday, only this time for definite."

"And just what was I saying? What did I tell you?" Fyodor asked, spreading his arms wide with a knowing smile.

* * *

The next day the pupils came to Maxim and Fyodor's place straight from work in order to discuss all the details, prepare themselves and draw up a precise plan.

Next Saturday Pyotr should have been working, but he'd arranged for a day off, even though he wasn't due for one. He'd had to wheedle and beg for it and make all sorts of promises. It had been particularly difficult to explain why he needed the day off: he couldn't tell them straight out he'd arranged to go to Pushkin, or they wouldn't have let him go! Go on Sunday instead, they'd have said. Vasilii didn't seem to have any problems, but you never knew where you were with his job; they could send him off on an assignment any day – although at least it was always just for one day.

They sat there for three hours hardly drinking anything at all, figuring out how much money they needed, what time they should leave and what they should take with them. Fyodor surprised everyone by getting very anxious and muttering: "Mustn't forget to take my coat, and take the padded jacket." He wanted everything thoroughly planned out and he got really fussy. He never usually bothered about anything – whether he had any money, whether the rent had been paid for, whether there was any food in the house – he couldn't care less; he always strolled around in the same clothes he slept in (he usually slept in his clothes).

But now he was like a completely different person. The trip to Pushkin seemed like something really special to him, a miraculous undertaking in which nothing could be left to chance. Maxim also behaved untypically – not using any expressions like "go fuck off", paying careful attention to everything, even allowing Fyodor to take his jacket. It was obvious that he and Fyodor had done a lot of talking even before the pupils arrived.

At last they decided: they'd buy the wine and food the next day, on Wednesday, to get the hassle over with. Pyotr would get the money for it – he'd sell some of his books on art during the lunch-break and immediately give the money to Maxim, who had volunteered to buy everything. With that settled, they all went their separate ways.

* * *

Not exciting enough? The sale of the books didn't go well – the shop only took half of them, so there obviously wasn't enough money. And on top of that Vasilii phoned Pyotr to say they were sending him on an assignment after all – but it was today, for one day, and he'd be back on Thursday evening, or Friday morning at the latest.

Maxim seemed really cut up by the news, although there obviously wasn't really anything to worry about – Vasilii would arrive on Friday and Pyotr would get the money tomorrow.

"That's not the problem," said Maxim, with a hopeless wave of his hand. "Fyodor'll be really upset, and anyway . . . it's all such a strain."

After lunch Vasilii phoned again to say he'd better not go anywhere, he'd ask a friend of his to go instead. That evening Pyotr naturally went to see Maxim and calm him down.

The atmosphere he found there was rather strained. The one thing capable of rejoicing the heart was the sight of Fyodor's jacket and coat, carefully folded up in the corner. For all the time he'd spent walking round the shops, Maxim hadn't managed to buy any port, which was so unusual he was furious. So far he'd only bought two bottles of vodka, and he and Fyodor had already downed one of them to steady their nerves. There was no point in reproaching them – Maxim was obviously suffering more than anyone else.

Pyotr suggested they should drop it, forget the whole thing, not in the sense that they shouldn't go to Pushkin at all – none of them could possibly think of doing that – but in the sense that they should put today's failures behind them and start again, making sure of everything, tomorrow: Pyotr would take in some books the shop was sure to buy, Maxim would just keep on searching until he found everything – it wasn't that difficult, they'd just been unlucky today.

After making this firm decision they felt a bit better and in their joy they saw off the second bottle of vodka.

*   *   *

Vasilii phoned again first thing in the morning and told them sullenly that his lousy friend couldn't be persuaded, and he was leaving right away, but he'd be there on Friday morning on the dot. Well, that wasn't really so bad.

Things went worse again with the sale of the books. The Bibliophile was closed for stocktaking that day.

"You rotten louse," yelled Maxim. "You blockhead, you spend days on end hanging about in that shop, couldn't you even remember when it's open?"

How could you explain to him? Pyotr phoned his work and told them he had to get a new passport urgently and he went off with Maxim to a different shop.

The place was packed solid. Maxim felt bad in the hot building, he had trouble breathing and kept wandering all over the place, until finally he got into an argument with a speculator in the passage outside. And all the time he seemed disgruntled about something.

"I'm selling my books, when I need them so badly, and he's not satisfied; yesterday he drank everything there was, and now he's not satisfied! I didn't try hard enough for him!" thought Pyotr, and to poison his spirit completely, he began picking over the books he'd brought to sell.

At long last they sold them and went out into the hot street.

"What use does Fyodor think he'll have there for his jacket?" asked Pyotr.

"To hell with him, let him lug the blasted jacket around, as long as he leaves the coat behind."

"He's not going to leave it, he'd rather hang himself. Listen, Maxim, let's decide that I won't come round this evening . . ."

"And why's that?"

"Because I've got work to do, a job! I'm already two hours late getting back from lunch break. I'll have to make it up this evening!"

"No need to yell like you're having a fit!"

"Okay . . . right then, on Friday, tomorrow, I'll come straight round after work, Vasilii too, and then first thing on Saturday . . ."

"Just you make sure you do!" Maxim said threateningly, turning sharply on his heels and limping away.

* * *

On Friday morning Vasilii phoned Pyotr long-distance and explained he was running around like a blue-arsed fly chasing everyone up, but none of them were doing bugger all; in short, he wouldn't arrive till late on Friday evening or maybe, at the latest, some time during the night. Pyotr starting swearing out loud in front of his workmates – his anxiety about Vasilii and Maxim had built up during the day because he didn't know whether Maxim had managed to buy anything.

They agreed Vasilii would leave that evening if it killed him, and if he didn't have time to wind things up down there, he'd just drop the whole damn job, even if it got him the sack.

Vasilii did try to hint they could go to Pushkin on Sunday instead, but Pyotr just howled and promised that now he'd punch Vasilii's face in for sure.

Vasilii didn't listen to him. He yelled back that in his place Pyotr would have topped himself, that he was busting a gut to get everything done down there so he could get back to Leningrad in time, but he was dealing with a load of shits down there . . . Pyotr put the phone down.

Pyotr's sweat hadn't even dried when the phone rang. It was Vasilii's wife (yes, strangely enough, Vasilii's married!), Lena, asking where Vasya was.

"What do you mean, where? He's at the whatsitsname, the drilling sites!"

"What? Well, if you say so. Sorry, I'm in a hurry, but anyway, if you see him before I do, tell him to come round to my place straight away. Got that? Straight away."

She rang off.

Pyotr leapt to his feet, ran to the mutual aid fund desk and borrowed a tenner in order to calm his panic and do at least something for the common cause, and like an idiot he bought three bottles of dry white (there wasn't any port).

* * *

That evening everything was fine. Pyotr, Maxim and Fyodor sat at the table like gentry, drinking a single bottle of dry wine.

The bag with the port, two bottles of dry wine and the salami was standing securely zipped up by the door.

But my God, what a morning it was! And, of course, it was raining. Pyotr kept wanting to dash out into the yard every minute to meet Vasilii, but Maxim forced him back down into his chair:

"D'you want to get lost too?"

Fyodor, who obviously hadn't slept all night, sat by the window as though he was waiting to be arrested – hunched over and twitching at the slightest sound. Maxim crossed his hands on his chest and fixed his eyes on the face of the clock borrowed specially from Kobot the day before.

The clock struck with inhuman ferocity.

The ring at the door eventually came, but it seemed unlikely to atone for the antecedent torment.

Vasilii burst into the flat like a hunted animal.

"Right! Let's go!" Maxim shouted immediately.

Everyone started dashing haphazardly round the room. Like a soldier at reveille, Fyodor rushed to put on his padded jacket.

"Stop! Let's sit in silence for a moment before the journey," said Pyotr on a sudden thought.

Everybody sat where they could. Vasilii, smiling blissfully, wiped away his sweat. Wasn't he a fine bastard!

"Okay, let's go."

They set off sedately down the stairs and across the yard, waving to the queue at the beer kiosk (need it be said that the entire queue had known about the trip to Pushkin since Tuesday?).

They waited till the bus arrived without feeling particularly impatient. The bus set off with a jolt and they all fell on top of each other, laughing happily, but Pyotr kept the bag pressed safely against his chest.

"Stop!" came a terrible cry from behind them – there was someone stumbling and weeping in the distance as he ran along after the bus. Fyodor hadn't got on.

* * *

There are actually people who are capable of not flinching under the blows of fate, like a stone bridge standing firm when the ice on the river breaks up.

And I suppose my Maxim must be one of them, even though he did get into a fight with the bus-driver so he refused to open the door at the next stop, and he vilified Vasilii for making the absurd assumption that Fyodor would realise he had to follow them, so perhaps they should wait for the next bus.

But then who else could have stopped the very first taxi without having any experience at all in such matters? No one but Maxim. Thus did Heracles halt the chariot of some queen on the edge of a precipice.

And who else could have found Fyodor, who'd gone to ground with all the artful ingenuity of an underground activist (Fyodor had missed his true vocation!) in the gap between the bus station and a building?

No, Maxim is just magnificent.

* * *

About two hours later they were walking along under the vaults of the Vitebsk Station. Moving in close order, holding each other by the shoulders and the arms, constantly glancing round and counting themselves, they got into the suburban train, then instantly went limp and slumped on to the seats like sacks of potatoes. They didn't feel like talking.

The train clattered on its way, and Fyodor pressed his face against the window, with his eyes roaming this way and that exactly like a little child. Everybody smiled and looked out through the window too.

"Well then, what about a drop of dry to celebrate?" asked Pyotr.

"Why not," said Maxim after short pause. "We could take a drop of the dry, seeing as it's such a big occasion. I didn't think we'd manage it. We were lucky, really lucky."

"Manage what?" enquired Pyotr.

"Going to Pushkin."

"Why wouldn't we manage it? What's strange is that we made such a cock-up of it!"

"You long streak of pseudo-Pelagian shit! When was the last time you ever managed anything?"

They took out a bottle of dry white, but no one had a knife. They were so unaccustomed to drinking dry wine that no one, not even Fyodor, had any real experience in opening that kind of bottle, with a cork.

"Hey, friend, you got a corkscrew on you?" Vasilii said to a man sitting nearby. He shook his head.

"Some kind of knife, then?"

The citizen hesitated for a moment, then took out a knife as slim as an awl.

Vasilii set about dealing with the cork, ripping pieces off it and trying to force it in, but it just wouldn't budge.

"I get out at the next step," said the citizen.

"Don't piss yourself, you'll make it," Maxim responded good-naturedly, sniffing in sage humour. He was clearly relaxed now, feeling his old self again.

Vasilii started hurrying and jabbing away with the knife as though he was mashing potatoes. Then one of his jabs missed and he stuck the knife into his wrist. A thin jet of blood struck the dusty ceiling.

"Hit a vein," Vasilii stated morosely. All the people sitting nearby started in fright and began staring in disgust. Some of them changed seats.

"You've got to get to the first aid point immediately!" shrieked the man who'd given them the knife. "Come on, don't just sit there!"

He was right. The train was standing at a station. It carried on standing there until there was an announcement:

"Comrades, please vacate the carriages. This train will not proceed any further."

* * *

When they got out at Pushkin the blood had stopped making new blotches on the handkerchief.

The sky was a solid mass of clouds and it was spitting with rain.

"You did right to bring your jacket, Fyodor," laughed Pyotr.

"Are we off to the park then?" asked Fyodor, glancing round.

"Of course," answered Maxim.

Everybody smiled.

HANGOVER

When Pyotr opened his eyes, it felt like he was reopening a half-healed wound.

"Are you going to work?" Maxim repeated.

"No," answered Pyotr, and pulled the coat up over his head.

Under the coat it was close and cosy, there was a smell of coarse tobacco, there was something spinning around in there. There seemed to be little creatures sitting in his fist and crawling in and out of it. They crawled as quick as they could, in case someone big, the size of a pig, came crawling through. Funny . . . why was everything so out of balance – his mouth was dry, on fire, but his feet were just the opposite, freezing cold? Because the head was more important? Or just closer? Or . . .

"Want some beer?" asked Maxim.

"No."

Several of the little people crawled into his fist at the same time. No, forget about work. Or . . . Ah, it was beer he was asking about: do I want some beer? Right, then!

He flung the coat aside and sat up.

"I've poured you some," said Maxim. "Go on, it'll steady you a bit."

It was a hazy morning; not in the sense that the room was filled with smoke, not that. In the slanting rays of the early light the bottles glinted like an aquarium, and everything white seemed hazy mother-of-pearly. Wasn't that wonderful – morning existed too. Pearly mother-of-morning. It wasn't beer he should be drinking, but coffee, as much as possible – and then set off walking and wondering.

Pyotr stood up, picked up his padded jacket off the floor then, not knowing where to put it and not capable of thinking the problem through, he dropped it again.

He put the glass to his lips and his teeth chattered against it.

There were so many things going on at every moment, his senses had become excessively heightened. Pyotr picked up his jacket again and was about to launch into God-knows-what far-reaching line of action, but he couldn't do it, he broke down and dropped it again.

He tried his beer again, too, gazing into the turbid depths of the sludge in a desperate search for hope, then groaning as he raised it to his lips and pressed them against it in a kiss. The beer seemed very thick, as though it wasn't even liquid. Drinking it immediately made him tired.

"The water's over there in the jar," said Maxim.

Pyotr staggered across, took a drink of water and staggered back.

"Listen, Maxim, I think I've got to go to the army office! Mobilisation registration certificate . . . registrificate!"

"Go on then, off you go."

Pyotr promptly swung round and tumbled out on to the street.

* * *

After walking about two hundred metres he halted and scrutinised the sky. Life hadn't really worked out, had it? A bit shattered. Everything smashed to pieces. Down the tubes. Pyotr laughed. Strange that his laugh sounded so carefree, so damned playful – and where could he have got such an idea right now?

He felt sad and weightless. Maybe he ought to have some coffee? No, there was nothing round here but lousy swill for twenty-two kopecks. He ought to eat something, though. Or go home? Home.

* * *

How happy that first half-hour at home is. You sit there on your own, eating, reading something or other, maybe even *The Literary Gazette*. Nothing happening, you're not taking anything in. And the price for half an hour out of your life is not worth worrying about, no more than a rouble – surely that can't be bad?

Pyotr covered up the dirty dishes with a rag that happened to come to hand and lay down on the sofa. Ran an eye over his books, had a smoke. Switched on the tape-deck, and even though he switched it off again immediately, Ellington's nervous rhythm had spoiled everything.

Pyotr came round for the second time that morning. Any minute now those little people would be creeping into his fist again. He had to start the day all over again. Or go to bed.

This wearisome, restless concern for the fate of the day! He ought to do something about it, if only to fill himself up with coffee or something.

He had to shake off this lethargy and for a start he could read Baudelaire's "The Voyage" at long last, calmly and without hurrying; he'd never found the time to do that. And if he didn't now, he never would because of this lethargic state.

> *For children crazed with maps and prints and stamps –*
> *The universe can sate their appetite.*
> *How vast the world is by the light of lamps,*
> *But in the eyes of memory how slight!*
>
> *One morning we set sail with brains on fire,*
> *And hearts swelled up with rancorous emotion,*
> *Balancing, to the rhythm of its lyre,*
> *Our infinite upon the finite ocean.*

From the very first lines Pyotr could tell this was the real thing. He was going to know these lines by heart and they would be his salvation in the jolting of the bus, and under the glaring daylight lamps at work; but before he'd even got half-way, he marked his place with a match and stuck the book in his briefcase – that wasn't it! Lovely poetry, but quicker, quicker, no time for wasting on poetry. What should he do?

The dust swirled slowly against the background of the window. It made the view out of the window of the pigeons and the fences seem like some magical, long-awaited film.

The Hermitage? The Hermitage!

Pyotr chuckled in stupefaction. How long was it since he'd been in the Hermitage, how long since he'd listened to that argument between delight and boredom in the face of his favourite portrait – the portrait of Jeremiah Decker?

Boredom had said: "Oh, how wearisome! Nothing but reprocessed waste – just how long can they go on sifting through it?"

Delight had said to his spouse: "Leave me be for an hour at least. Stop foisting that accursed novelty of yours on me, I'm not dead yet!"

No, for the Hermitage you had to be in harmony with yourself. But what about everything else? What a drag it was, this presentiment of some better fate! Was this really the life a man was born for, wanting to be serious and solemn and never, but never, achieving it, not even for a minute, even though it was dangling right there, just out of reach?

Or am I the only one? Or am I just incapable of loving anyone?

* * *

As he'd already done once that day, Pyotr literally tumbled out into the street, in a state of nostalgic and fruitless distraction. He sat down on a bench and put his hand in his pocket, thrusting his fingers into the accumulated mass of tobacco crumbs. It was like pushing your hand into warm sand – no, into warm seawater, when you were still light-headed after bathing in it.

What about the sand? The wet sand, slowly solidifying into towers, terrible towers like Antonio Gaudì's. Far, far away. And the sun receding and shrinking too.

Pyotr scooped out a handful of tobacco and swung his hand through the air. A spray of brown powder, like that time out of the window.

The pigeons flew up into the air, but immediately settled back down, thinking they'd been thrown something to eat. Shoo, pigeons, shoo.

And why shoo? What a word – shoo! Eh? Shoo, shoo! That's what she'd said when he'd reached out and tried to kiss her.

Yes, by the way, that's what he ought to do! Phone someone, Lizaveta, maybe, and take her down the bar for a beer! Sad and weightless. Unfortunately I don't drink. Ever.

And anyway, darling Lizaveta . . .

Vasilii was right when he said the devil knows how to make the memory of those minutes when we do evil pleasant. Sad and weight-less. It was true, true; better for me to suffer alone than . . . But what was evil about it? Where was the sin? Vivekananda was right when he said that sin consists in thinking of yourself or another as commit-ting sin. What would that dualist Vasilii say to that? But no, he was right. He was right, and so was the other. And all the rest of them. Had he tried the lot? No more, no more! Better puke it all up than turn into a professional taster!

* * *

Pyotr kept walking faster and faster, glancing anxiously at the cinema posters. God forbid he should end up there!

But then, for only forty kopecks you could forget all about life for an hour and a half.

Cheap. But cheap stuff only makes the hangover worse.

What advantages the cinema had over life! Everything in it moved fast, even if it wasn't interesting, and most important of all, it had musical accompaniment.

What music, accompanying what? Where am I going? What dif-ference does it make what kind of accompaniment it has? Music, freedom, peace. Even in prison. I don't want a million, I just want to resolve an idea, but how can you resolve it if you can't grasp it in your hand, and even if you catch it, it's like a slippery fish – one flip and it's back in the river.

"Hey, you lad, hang on!" a ragged-looking man called out to Pyotr.

"What?"

"Don't be in such a rush. You going to the army office?"

"No," replied Pyotr, astonished because he really did have to go to the army office, only not in this district.

"Oh, okay. I thought you was going to the army office. Give me eleven kopecks, I'll get a small one at least."

Pyotr gave him the money and set off even faster, knowing where he was going now.

* * *

It was getting near evening. People had already left work and were standing in their queues – some in shops, some in the crush out on the street.

Pyotr stood hunched over beside a street kiosk, observing the rapid and infernal movement of the herrings on the counter, the people and the automobiles. Everything, even the herrings, looked so intense, as though it had just torn itself away from its real, genuine business for a quick dash across to some other genuine business.

Pyotr wanted to grab one of these men by the lapels of his jacket and shout with all his strength: "News! Give me news!"

Didn't Vonnegut have a phrase like that somewhere? Always there's that reflex of awareness; rails where there's no track.

Life just seems quite impossible – don't be daft, it goes on. We carry on living. There's the sun already down between the houses: the final slanting, Dostoevskian rays.

The more pain I feel, the better. Why? Why should my conscience, which probably doesn't even exist, torment me for God knows what?

Or maybe Vasilii's right! It's the sense of original sin, and let's just leave it at that? Maybe it's just my sins tormenting me?

At least Vasilii can atone for his sins in prayer, but then what does that mean, atone? All you can do is put them right, but then you can't do that either.

You can buy an indulgence at the Delicatessen. For two forty-two. Or four twenty.

Obviously there's no grace for me, none. And without it life's just an empty word. Just like in the cinema – cover the opening the light comes through and the screen's empty, nothing but dialogue. Nothing but dialogue. You can only live in God's beam of light. Living outside that light requires such an effort. And anyway . . . No matter what effort a figure on the screen made when the little window was curtained off, there was no way it was going to survive.

But what if it could, after all? What if it could, Lord?

Oh, what a whinger I am! What shall I do, what shall I do? What should I be, and who's to blame? Look at that old man crossing the street, it's difficult for him! Why don't you help him?

Pyotr flung one arm out wildly, spat and dashed across the street. Without even slowing his pace, he barged into the door of a bar. It didn't budge.

The doorman stared at him, fish-eyed.

"Let me in, I say," shouted Pyotr.

* * *

"You know," said Maxim as he opened the door, "Fyodor's sick."

"Sick? What's wrong with him?" Pyotr asked in surprise.

"God only knows. Don't reckon he's ever been sick before."

"Has he got a temperature? Has he got any pain?"

"Kobot says he's got a temperature. He doesn't say anything. We started playing cards and I saw he couldn't. Half-dead, he was."

Pyotr quickly went through into the room as though he were apologising for something, and sat down on the floor beside Fyodor's folding bed.

"What's wrong, Fyodor?"

"I feel sort of sick. I could do with some port, but he said there's no money."

"I haven't got any either." Pyotr rummaged guiltily in trouser pockets he already knew were empty. "Did you take any aspirin?"

"Kobot gave me something."

"Sleep, that's what you need. Did you sleep today?"

"All day long."

"That's all right then, tomorrow you'll feel better. Or we could call a doctor."

"No, don't. I'd rather feel better tomorrow."

"Bugger the doctor," said Maxim, coming into the room. "I called a doctor once – afterwards there's all sorts of hassle, and it's just a waste of time. Kobot knows what he's doing, he gave him these tablets."

"Which ones? Show me."

"They're over there on the floor."

There were packets of aspirin and barbamil lying on the floor.

"I'll bring some more tomorrow, different ones," said Maxim, "and anyway, stop worrying, will you? Maybe he's not really sick at all, just ate some fish that disagreed with him."

Pyotr turned over the tablets and the magazines on the floor and picked up the notebook in which Fyodor occasionally wrote down whatever he felt like writing – things he made up, or things he heard.

He looked at the latest entries:

If a man eats in the dark, even if they call him a night-feeder, it's all right.

* * *

Like is dissimilar to like.

* * *

You have to be very clear about your reasons for not drinking.

* * *

There may be clever people about, but it makes no difference.

* * *

Draught's cheaper, and you don't have to take the bottles back.

* * *

You have to trust life, it's smarter. Even accept that however things
turn out, it's okay.

* * *

Are you hoping that however things turn out it'll be okay? That
means the devil will make your choice for you.

ON THE DEATH OF A FRIEND

The truck came down along the street,
Knocked Nikolai right off his feet!

"Hey now! When did you write all that?" asked Pyotr.
"He did that today," Maxim answered proudly.
"And the poem's today's too?"
"The poem too."
Pyotr slapped himself on the forehead and took a book out of his
briefcase.
"Now listen carefully and don't interrupt."
Fyodor sat up and lowered his bare feet on to the floor, Maxim
frowned slightly. They both lit up.

For children crazed with maps and prints and stamps –

RETURN FROM JAPAN

Maxim and Fyodor were sitting, leaning against each other, in a small clearing covered with a thick layer of aluminium bottle-caps; the caps covered this magical spot in a layer several centimetres thick that glittered gold and silver like precious jewels.

At the edge of the clearing there were frozen splashes and waves of multi-coloured splinters of glass. It was a shame to leave, but the train would be there soon.

Fyodor had long since lost his bearings and had no idea where to go, in which direction, what for, but none the less Maxim had insisted on going back. At least they didn't have to think about that, the going back; it was gradually happening of its own accord – either they managed to get a lift in a truck going their way, or they fell asleep drunk in some goods train, and it always carried them in the right direction, towards Europe.

The return was unhurried, almost involuntary – as if Maxim and Fyodor were leaning with their backs against some barrier and the barrier was slowly moving back, gradually overcoming the inertia of repose.

* * *

"Maxim, didn't you say something about a train?" asked Fyodor.

Maxim lifted his head a little and dropped it again.

Fyodor had no need of a train; he wasn't suffering from either despair or impatience, he wasn't trying to guess the future and he wasn't afraid of it. But since Maxim had mentioned a train . . .

"Hey son, what's your name, help me get Maxim to the train," said Fyodor, appealing to the guy lying opposite, a chance drinking-companion.

The guy looked up at Fyodor through dull, unseeing eyes devoid of expression: "Did you rattle your face?"

"I've got to get Maxim down there."

"Down where?"

"To the train."

"Need a ticket. You got a ticket?"

"Maxim said you'd got the ticket, you bought it. Remember?"

The other guy turned out his pockets.

"What ticket, you numbskull? Ain't no ticket here."

But then two tickets fell out of his pocket.

Fyodor picked up the tickets and shoved them into Maxim's pocket, then took Maxim under the arms and dragged him towards the long platform that was visible through the bushes.

The young guy started staggering after them, but after a few steps he dropped to his knees and stopped moving.

Gasping for breath and almost fainting, Fyodor reached the edge of the track and miraculously – someone obviously helped him – shoved Maxim into the lobby of a carriage and slumped down beside him like a soldier who has crawled over the parapet with a wounded comrade to the safety of the trench.

Someone shook him, asking questions and making suggestions – Fyodor said nothing and didn't move.

* * *

When he woke up, Maxim was no longer there beside him.

The train was moving fast, the doors of the lobby were banging and rattling.

Fyodor got to his feet. Glancing out in terror at the blackness beyond the window, he went through timidly into the carriage with its smell of suffocating hopelessness. Maxim wasn't there, there was no one there at all apart from a woman in a greasy dressing-gown and hideous shiny stockings. She studied Fyodor with hatred and curiosity.

Fyodor slammed the door shut. He stood there uncertainly, grimacing in the draught, then he opened the outside door and jumped out of the train.

His body bounced lightly off the embankment and went hurtling
into the alder bushes.

* * *

The noise of the train had already faded away when Fyodor recovered, got to his feet and started clumsily up the stony embankment
towards the damp glimmering of the sleepers and the lamp.

Although it was already getting light, he couldn't see the small
stones crunching under his shoes, his feet kept sliding apart and sink-
ing into the slippery mess.

After he'd walked about a hundred metres, Fyodor climbed down
the embankment, parted the wet bushes with his hands and set off,
almost in tears, in a direction perpendicular to the railway line.

The forest exuded the gravity of the hour before dawn; it was quiet.

It looked as though things might turn out badly.

PART THREE

APOCRYPHAL MATERIAL CONCERNING MAXIM AND FYODOR

THE YOUTH OF MAXIM
(materials for a biography)

By the time Maxim turned twenty he was already turning out plays at a spanking pace: he had already written and recorded his own renditions of the following plays: *The Three Cognacs, Bakunin, Icarus Lost, The Pursuer, A Trip to the Country, Andrei Andreevich, Beer for the Monk, The Golem* and others.

As Maxim's acquaintances recall, the plays were apparently not too bad, but no one can remember what they were about.

Fyodor, who knew Maxim at that time, claims that the plays were brilliant, but he has said very little concerning their actual content; we may assume that they were narratives concerning certain villages and drinking companions who had disappeared, and about Fyodor during his schooldays.

Maxim's former wife also confirmed that the plays were brilliant, stating that the play *Icarus Lost* was about Icarus and the play *Bakunin* was about Bakunin. Her testimony is clearly reliable, since it is she who keeps the tapes on which the plays were recorded. (Unfortunately these tapes were subsequently used to record Abba and Boney M tracks.)

Maxim's former wife has fond memories of the evenings when Maxim's friends listened to the plays. The atmosphere was natural and unconstrained and wine was purchased; everyone wanted to relax and enjoy themselves, and a humorous remark, which later became a popular catchphrase, was frequently uttered: "Maxim, why don't you stick your bloody plays up your arse!"

Although writing the plays took up a great deal of Maxim's time, he had a job – evidently for the purpose of gathering material for literary use – as a junior accountant in an office.

In the light of the fact that in his free time Maxim did the housekeeping and also that he made frequent mention of his desire to become a yard-keeper, one cannot but recall the words of Marx and Engels in their work *The German Ideology:* "In communist society, where no one is restricted to any exclusive area of activity, everyone can perfect himself in any area . . . do one thing today and another tomorrow, go hunting in the morning, fishing in the afternoon, raise cattle in the evening and after supper devote myself to criticism, or whatever my heart desires."

In the full sense of the word Maxim was not restricted to any exclusive area of activity. Thus, at the age of twenty-two, to the surprise of his friends he abandoned both his literary and accounting activities and spent two years perfecting himself exclusively in the military arena – and not as a dilettante, but in the ranks of the armed forces.

Such are the few known details of the early life of Maxim, prior to his divorce from his wife; the remaining information is extremely fragmented and contradictory; his former wife, for instance, claims that as the years went by he became ever more morose and anxious, would not spend the night at home and avoided his friends, but Fyodor claims that it was quite the opposite, that Maxim "just gave up worrying about things".

It is simply not possible to grasp the meaning of such contradictory assessments.

Maxim himself never talks about his young days, and when asked about the formative influences on his character he merely gazes sadly out of the window.

THUS SPAKE MAXIM

1

Maxim rose in the middle of the night to get a drink of water from the tap, and after slaking his thirst he sat down at the table for a breather.

Grunting as he started to get up, he spied a box there on the table, with lettering on it that said: "To Maxim from Pyotr."

And when he opened up the box, inside it was a pair of brown shoes from the FastFoot factory.

Maxim gave a wan laugh and began wondering whether he should go back to bed or take another drink of water.

And he said: "Pyotr, what do you, the only person who remembers my birthday, expect from me? Gratitude? You know the way I express my most heartfelt gratitude: go stick your brown shoes up your arse.

"But don't you worry, you won't receive that kind of thanks from me. For even in this world each should be recompensed according to his true intent; so here is my reward for you.

"In very truth, it were better for you to believe that I utter these words on autopilot!"

2

"Yes, you guessed right, I am a tender-hearted and nostalgic soul – is that not what you wanted to stir up again? Did you notice that at New Year I just can't bear to be out on the streets and I send Fyodor to the shop? I simply cannot stand the sight of my strangled childhood in those thousands of bright, twinkling New Year trees.

"Do you know what your present is? A flower cast in the path of a runner! Even on a flower you can slip and fall, and where's the sense in it? Of what use is an aspirin to Socrates after he's drunk the hemlock?" Thus spake Maxim.

3

"Yea, verily have I turned my blood to poison and I give it to you: take and drink; and you want to give me an aspirin?

"I am he that prepares the way for the Reaper. I teach you to die and to fertilise the soil for those that come after the Reaper – and not be mown down like the common trash beneath his sickle.

"Your father and your mother both quaffed poisoned wine to the thunder of marching tunes, and your first cry upon emerging from your mother's womb was the cry of a drunken man.

"You murmur against God, asking why will he not set aside the lid of the coffin which is your life.

"But then will you not suffer still more grievously on finding that you cannot rise up in your drunken state?

"You are kind and thoughtful only in that you are feeble and drunk. Oh, do not at least give this the name of virtue!

"Do you know what is done with a tree that brings forth no fruit? The Good Gardener will heap the soil up on it full seventy times seven.

"But what, say, can be done with a withered tree?

"Will the Reaper pass you by? The movement of your life is but the constant turning of a single circle: the vomit of remorse after the wine of debauchery.

"But what of the wine of debauchery! All poison is become meat and drink to you now: I fear I have come too late in your evolution with my pure poison.

"And yet you are the best of all this common trash!

"The setting sun has tainted all that's best in you – but the burden of sunset is no justification – neither Walsingham nor Venya with his transpierced throat shall wheedle a postponement from the Reaper!"

Thus spake Maxim; and in speaking he did waken Fyodor, who emerged into the kitchen in his long-johns and sat down facing Maxim without a word.

And Maxim did pour the port.

MAXIM AND FYODOR:
THE CORRESPONDENCE

Hello, dear Maxim!

I reached the village okay. My brother's glad to see me, he's really good and kind. I want to make a suggestion: don't throw all my letters away, put them in the dresser and I won't throw yours away either.

Then I won't just have a "Notebook", I'll have a "Correspondence with Friends" too, and afterwards I can keep a "Writer's Diary".

That's all I've got to write about.

Goodbye for now, Fyodor.

* * *

Hello, dear Maxim!

There's something I forgot to write: after I got here, the next day I said to my brother, let's go to the shop. But the thing he told me was: there isn't any shop in their village, or in the next one – there's only one in Ozhogin Volochok, and there's no moonshine either.

I asked him: how can you live here like that? And he told me all the guys get together and go to Ozhogin Volochok for the whole day, and if there's nothing there, they keep on walking until night, with the guys from the other villages.

Then I said to him: right, let's go. We went to Ozhogin Volochok with rucksacks like all the guys here keep specially.

That's all I've got to write about.

Goodbye for now, Fyodor.

* * *

Hello, Fyodor!

Mm . . . bugger off.

* * *

Hello, dear Maxim!

I'm still amazed at the important fact that there's no shop in our village. A lot of the guys die the next morning or kill themselves because of it. Because they can't walk a long way.

And on their graves they write: "Died of a hangover."

The background to all this is that there's no sobering-up station here. So you can walk around outside as much as you like.

I got your letter. Write again.

That's all I've got to write about.

I miss you very much; I bow down three times to the damp mother earth at your feet.

Goodbye for now. Fyodor.

* * *

Hello, Fyodor!

I can't write, I've got a terrible hangover.

Now I've recovered, I feel better.

* * *

Hello, my dear Maxim!

Everybody here loves me because I'm from the city. I've written out my poem "On the Death of a Friend" for lots of the guys as a keepsake. If you don't remember it, I can remind you:

ON THE DEATH OF A FRIEND

The truck came down along the street,
Knocked Nikolai right off his feet

The guys here are all nice and kind. I read them your letters and they liked them.

"Whoah," they say, "we know all about hangovers . . . But

Maxim's feeling better, he must be okay!" But they say my letters read better.

I've taught them to do something: not to walk back home from Ozhogin Volochok, but drink everything there. At night we light bonfires, I teach them Zen Buddhism and we sing songs. And in the morning, there's the shop!

That's all I've got to write about.

I bow low at your feet.

Goodbye for now, Fyodor.

* * *

Hello, Fyodor!

I don't feel up to writing, so Vasilii will write for me.

Hello, Fyodor!

I read your letters with interest – and I remembered Andrei Bely's verse:

Yesterday he called into a tavern
And drank his monthly earnings down
Today he walks home to his native village,
Bowed by the distance to the very ground.

And later:

Cold and hunger lie in wait, believe me!
Jail and ruin lie just up ahead.
The vodka burns brutal and savage,
Enflaming his heart and his head!

But, God knows, things are even worse now! And everywhere, it seems!

The whole country – but what country? There is no country! The whole people is degenerating to the very point of extinction.

Drunken tears have flooded all the straight paths and they are on the verge of being transformed into bogs.

"Prepare ye the ways of the Lord and make ye them straight!" but how, exactly? "Everyone is covered in vomit and everyone is oppressed and suffering, sound all the bells and no one will even raise his head . . ." as the great classic wrote. Surely now things are worse? Everyone is covered in vomit and everyone is having A GOOD TIME, everyone is in a state of blissful, drunken hope, a rainbow-coloured artificial sky has been erected above hell.

Oh well . . . Goodbye for now. Vasilii.

* * *

Hello, my dear Maxim!

I received your and Vasilii's letter. Thank you, Vasilii, write more often.

I'm enjoying life here. We've made ourselves a little dug-out in the forest close to Ozhogin Volochok. Some of the guys from Ozhogin Volochok share the dug-out with us and we get along like great friends.

I've written a poem that they recite to any women who come to our dug-out. Here is the poem:

TO THE UNKNOWN WOMAN

Get away!
Shove off!

There's another version too:

TO THE UNKNOWN WOMAN

Get away!
Fuck off!

But I haven't told any of the guys the second version, it would be a bit awkward.

That's all I have to write about.

Goodbye for now. Fyodor.

* * *

Hello, dear Maxim!

I'll do whatever you write, I don't know what to do myself. Now I'll tell you everything just the way it was.

The guys and me went to the shop in the morning and one guy, Nikolai (he's a nice guy, kind), said: "Aunty Masha! Give us ten bottles of snout-twister."

Then suddenly the shop woman said: "No more! Yesterday the chairman came round, and said: 'Hay-making's started. Don't let them have any more!' And they're not going to bring any more in until hay-making's done."

Nikolai said: "Never mind the hay-making, just give us some snout-twister."

She said to him: "No more!"

So then Nikolai put this idea to her: "It'd be better, you bad bitch, if the chairman had told you: 'Shoot the lot of them, hay-making's started!'"

But she said to him: "Go away, Nikolai, you're not wearing a cross – you unholy devil!"

Then all the guys started pushing me forward – tell her, they said, you're from the city.

And just when I was going to tell her what I thought, she said: "And I've no time for that city-man of yours! He's the one who brought you down so low, it's his fault you went to live in that dug-out!"

Maxim! Maxim! I felt so terribly ashamed, I even covered my face with my hands and went out of the shop on to the porch.

Then all the guys came out too and we just set off along the road.

Send me a telegram, Maxim.

That's all I have to write about.

I bow down low three times at your feet.

Goodbye for now. Fyodor.

* * *

Fyodor, stop wasting your bloody time down there, come back!
Maxim.

* * *

Hello, dear Maxim!

I got your telegram, thanks.

You know, Maxim, I've been thinking and I don't see how I can
bring all the guys back with me, because we probably won't be able
to move all of them into our room, we won't fit in (or maybe we
could, somehow); and if we dig a dug-out in our yard, it'll be too cold
in winter.

So I can't come back just yet. I'll stay here and think what to do.

Goodbye for now. Fyodor.

FYODOR'S DIARY

1 March

Today is 1 March. I've decided to keep a diary as well as my note-books. We drank to the idea.

2 March

I can't remember a thing that happened. It's a pity, I wanted to record everything in detail.

3 March

Today I go into the toilet and there written on the wall is: "Agapov was here." I ask Maxim: "Maxim, who's this guy Agapov who's been here?"

Then Maxim tells me that yesterday we had a visitor called Agapov. He talked about the war and I wrote it all down and I even cried. So I take a look and right there in my notebook it says:

"I served in Germany, in this base that was built back under the Germans. So one day there I am on duty in the mess hall; the first shift's already had lunch and we're laying everything out for the second shift and clearing away the dishes, when suddenly this German from the farm that was near the base comes running in. 'I've got to see the commanding officer of the unit!' he says. 'Get me the commanding officer.'

"Well anyway, we thought it over, then we called the commanding officer. And then this German tells him there's this German archive left on his farm, and in this archive there's this document that says this mess hall of ours is mined and set to explode at lunch-time today. Can you imagine that? That very same mess hall we're standing in that very moment, and the Germans mined it twenty years ago and the bastards deliberately set it to blow up during lunch!

"Well anyway, the commanding officer thought it over, and he ordered everyone out of the mess hall. And no sooner have we all gone outside than there's this almighty ker-boom! Not a trace left of the mess hall, and it was a fair old size, half a kilometre long it was, they couldn't find so much as a stone the size of this cork. Nothing left but this crater about a hundred metres across.

"Well anyway, we levelled out the crater, cleaned everything out of the way and built a new mess hall on the same site.

"So what d'you reckon? Six months goes by and the mess hall gets blown to buggery again! That's the way those bastard Germans mined things when they were retreating!"

It turns out that's the story Agapov told me. After I read it I went straight out to the shop.

4 March
Today's Saturday. So we drank to that.

5 March
Somehow today I fancied a drink from first thing.

Never put off, as they say . . . so we went at it and drank with gusto. (Note from Vasilii: Fyodor, why do you copy out such long stories from your notebook? And apart from that, write more clearly: for instance, instead of the expression "we drank with gusto", you could write "I laid out my lunch" or "I puked my guts up".)

6 March
Had a bet with Vasilii about whether you can guzzle enough Merlot white to switch into autopilot. He said you can't, but it didn't take me long to win.

7 March
Tomorrow's 8 March, Women's Day. So we drank to that.

8 March
We drank to 8 March.

9 March
We drank to 9 March.

10 March
Vasilii brought some moonshine and Pyotr brought some snout-twister. We make cocktails. They turned out quite nice.

11 March
Today we bought six bottles of snout-twister. And polished them all off.

12 March
It's already the middle of March, but it's still cold. To warm us up we drank one bottle of snout-twister.

13 March
Today's Sunday. We had trouble getting any snout-twister.

14 March
This morning Maxim called me in a weak little voice: "Fyodor! Fyo-odor!" I went and I said: "What is it, Maxim lad?"

And he said to me: "Let's snort a drop of snout-twister!" I didn't object.

15 March
Vasilii came round, and right there in the doorway I said to him: "*Basille! Snout-twister ou la mort?*"*

He went pale and said: "Snout-twister."**

I said to him: "That's right!"

---

*Vasilii! Snout-twister or death! (Fr.)

**Snout-twister (Fr.)

16 March
This morning when Vasilii got up to go to work he staggered and fell.
I ran to phone Pyotr: "Pyotr!" I said, "Come quick, Vasilii's not well!"

Pyotr was frightened. He asked: "What should I get, port or snout-twister?"

I said: "Get some snout-twister!" I put the phone down and ran.

17 March
Today I said to Maxim: "Maxim, if we drink snout-twister again today, we'll get ill."

He agreed. We drank port.

18 March
This morning I said to Maxim: "Maxim, you do what you like, but I won't try to pretend – today I've decided to get plastered!"

Maxim slapped me on the shoulder and said: "Me too!"

19 March
I don't remember a thing that happened.

20 March
I don't remember a thing.

21 March
Maxim's a nice guy, of course, but today he really insulted me.

I finally told him I wanted to be a cosmonaut and he really insulted me. I was so hurt I had to drown my grief in drink.

22 March
Maxim's in a bad mood again today. He was cursing so badly Pyotr said to him: "Maxim, don't get so agitated, nerve cells don't regenerate."

But Maxim gave him a wild glance and yelled: "Good riddance to that shit!"

Then he grabbed this 33 per cent port and swigged down the whole bottle. We hadn't even reached autopilot before he switched off.

23 March
Today Maxim woke up and just kept staring out of the window. I
started staring out of the window too – outside it was sunny and
warm like in the countryside or when I used to go to school. It used
to be warm like that.

I said to Maxim: "Maxim, look how warm it is, how fine! All the
birdies and beasties are happy, they're singing because they've sur-
vived the winter, and winter's over. How beautiful the trees are today,
look! And what I want to say to you, Maxim is: don't drink for a
whole year, even for two, but God made today for drinking!"

But Maxim just looked out of the window and said: "We're not
going to drink today."

"What, Maxim, nothing at all?"

"Nothing at all, Fyodor."

"What about tomorrow then?"

1980

NOTES
FOR *MAXIM AND FYODOR*

by Vladimir Shinkarev

Page 11

Dedication

KONSTANTINOV, Igor: a little-known Soviet Russian poet, artist and musician, V. Shinkarev's teacher.

Epigraph

PLATONOV, Andrei Platonovich (1899–1951): a Soviet Russian writer. The epigraph is taken from Platonov's most important work, the novel *Djan* (1934).

Page 13

MAXIM (from the Latin *maxima sententia* – the highest principle): a brief dictum expressing a principle of moral or social conduct in a concise form. Similar to aphorism.

LAWS OF DIALECTICS: the unity and struggle of opposites, the transformation of quantitative changes into qualitative and the negation of the negation make up the most important part of dialectics, which is the theory and method of the cognition of reality in the process of its dynamic development, a branch of philosophy which deals with the most general laws of the development of nature, society and thought; dialectics is opposed to metaphysics.

Page 14

BOOKS WHICH ARE BEST NOT DISCUSSED WITH PEOPLE YOU DON'T KNOW VERY WELL: literature which during "the period of stagnation" was regarded as anti-Soviet: for instance, *Maxim and Fyodor*.

Page 15

BEER IS MADE UP OF OF ATOMS: many items consist of atoms, including beer. In terms of increasing quality beer is divided into canned (in 3.5-litre cans or larger), bottled (0.5 litres) and canned again (0.33 litres).

AESOP: an Ancient Greek fabulist (6th century BC) who is regarded as the founder of the genre of the fable.

MOLECULAR STRUCTURE: numerous items also consist of molecules.

ESCAPISM (from the verb "escape', meaning "to flee from danger", "to save oneself"): an attempt by the individual to withdraw from reality into a world of illusion and fantasy.

Page 17

GARDEN OF STONES (philosophical garden, garden of Reanji): a deliberately composed arrangement of 15 rocks in the Monastery of Reanji (Kyoto, Japan), 15th century. Created by Soami. The stones are arranged in such a way that it is only possible to view 14 of them at any one time. A spot for solitary contemplation.

HAIKU: a genre of Japanese poetry. An unrhymed triplet consisting of 17 syllables (5-7-5). Distinguished by the simplicity of its poetic language and freedom of expression.

TANKA (short song): a genre of Japanese poetry. An unrhymed quintuplet consisting of 31 syllables (5+7+5+7+7). Distinguished by its poetic elegance and laconicism.

TANK: an armoured military vehicle running on caterpillar tracks. First used by English forces in 1916 during the First World War.

ARMOURED CAR (or personnel carrier): an armoured military vehicle running on caterpillar tracks or wheels which is used for transporting armed soldiers to the battlefield and providing them with covering fire. First appeared in Great Britain in 1918.

BLOOMING (BLOSSOMING) CHERRY (sakura): a decorative species of cherry. The cherry tree is the national symbol of Japan. Its fruits are not edible.

KYOTO: a city of the island of Honshu (Japan), until 1868 the capital of Japan.

MIKASA, KASUGA, AVADZA, INAMIDZUMA, TAGO: towns in Japan.

RYABOVO, RZHEVKA, GRIVA, PISKARYOVKA, VSEVOLOZHSK: towns and villages in the Leningrad Region (more specifically, stops on the railway line to Irinovo).

PETROKREPOST: a town in the Leningrad Region. Until 1611 known as Oreshek, from 1702 to 1944 as Schlusselberg.

LAMPED: struck (vern.).

Page 18

SAKE: Japanese rice wine.

ZEN BUDDHISM: see note to page 23.

MAXIM STOOD WITH HIS FINGER RAISED: this haiku describes a koan that is widely used in the practice of Zen – a finger suddenly raised instead of an answer to a question may lead to satori.

Page 19

MATTING: here, a densely interwoven mat of straw, rushes or grass. The peoples of Asia use such matting for sitting on.

SLUMPED STRAIGHT DOWN ON TO THE MATTING: in early versions "collapsed on the tatami".

TATAMI: a Japanese mat made of straw. In sport, a resilient mat used for judo (1.4 x 1.4 m).

RANSETSU (1652–1707): a Japanese poet, a pupil of Basho.

INWARD CONTEMPLATION: the same as meditation, a specific individual psychological activity which is intended to achieve a deepened state of awareness. Widespread in Zen as a means of withdrawal from the empirical world. Typically accompanied by physical relaxation and the absence of external displays of emotion.

FUJI: Fujiyama, an active volcano on the island of Honshu (3,776 m.) A sacred mountain to the Japanese. A favourite subject in Japanese art.

HOKUSAI, Katsushika (1760–1849): a Japanese painter and draughtsman, a master of colour printmaking. A member of the Ukiyo-e school.

EMERALD GLINT OF JASPER: wine and beer bottles of the time described were made of semi-transparent green glass.

Page 20
HARA-KIRI (from the Japanese "hara", meaning "belly", and "kiri",
meaning "to cut"): a ritual form of suicide practised in samurai circles and
performed by ripping open the belly. It could be imposed as a sentence or
committed voluntarily.
AKUTAGAVA RUNOSKE (1892–1927): a Japanese writer.

Page 21
FYODOR'S SLEEVES WERE WET: the tear-soaked sleeves of the kimono of a
woman in distress are one of the traditional images of Japanese poetry.

Page 23
ZEN: the Japanese equivalent of the Chinese "Chan', from the Sanskrit
"Dhan". In Hinduism and Buddhism it signifies focused attention or
meditation (see note to page 19). Zen Buddhists link dhan with the practice
of "satori" – sudden enlightenment – and the manifestation of the wisdom of
the Buddha in the transformed consciousness of the individual. Typified by
alogicality and contempt for the external forms of individual existence.
Founded by the Indian Buddhist missionary Boddidharma (6ᵗʰ century BC).
KOAN: "The system which is presently used by most followers of Zen.
In literal terms koan means a well-known public document, which the
Teacher uses in an attempt to test the depth of his pupil's understanding."
(Dr Daisetsu T. Suzuki in his book *Zen Living*, London, 1950.)
BODHISATTVA: the first patriarch of Zen in China, who first brought the idea
of Zen from India in the early 6ᵗʰ century.
WHAT IS THE MEANING OF THE ADVENT OF THE BODHISATTVA OF
THE SOUTH: a question similar in meaning to the question "What is the
meaning of Zen Buddhism?"
GO FUCK YOURSELF: a paradoxical and illogical reply to a question,
possibly even a blow with a stick, provides the almost compulsory conclusion
to a Zen Buddhist fable.

Page 24
DAISETSU SUZUKI (1869–1966): a Japanese scholar and philosopher, a
promoter of Zen Buddhism in Japan and Europe, the author of dozens of
books on Zen. He was not a member of any of the Japanese schools of
Buddhism, but he is revered in Japan as an enlightened Buddhist.
FETCHED HIM A WALLOP: struck (vulg.).
FETCHED HIM A WALLOP ACROSS HIS BAD EAR: this fable recalls an
utterance of one of the Zen patriarchs: "If I met the Buddha, I would bash his
head in."
DISCOVERED WITHIN HIMSELF THE COURAGE NOT TO RECTIFY
HIS ERROR: "Having committed an error, have the courage not to correct it"
– an aphorism of I. Konstantinov, whose world view in 1980 diverged only

slightly from Zen Buddhism.
HE HAD STUFFED THE CAT INTO AN EMPTY GLASS JAR: this fable is
associated with one of the famous traditional ones:

A pupil asked: "A gosling was put into a jug. He grew into a goose that could
not pass through the mouth of the jug. How can he be taken out without
breaking the jug?"
    Instead of replying, the teacher shouted out the pupil's name loudly.
    "I'm here!" responded the pupil.
    "There," the teacher remarked calmly, "the goose is already free."
    The pupil experienced enlightenment.

Page 26
A QUARTER BOTTLE: a bottle of vodka which holds 0.25 litres.

Page 27
MONOGATARI (tale): a genre of Japanese narrative literature. In the wider
sense a novella or novel, in the narrower sense works of the 9th to 16th centuries.
CLEOPATRA (69–30 BC): the final queen of Egypt (from 51 BC) from the
Ptolemy dynasty (see A.S. Pushkin's *Egyptian Nights*).
WIPED DOWN A BOTTLE: bottles of wine were delivered to shops from the
alcohol and vodka factories in crates filled with wood shavings.

Page 32
REPIN, Ilya Efimovich (1844–1930): Russian artist, a member of the
"Wanderers" group. Painted *The Volga Boatmen* (1870–3). A master
draughtsman.
OTTOMAN: a form of divan.

Page 33
CARNET, Marcel (born 1909): a French film director. His film *Daybreak*
(1939) shows the tragic isolation of man in a world dominated by betrayal and
base motivation.

Page 34
THE LAY OF MY MAXIM: a stylistic imitation of *The Lay of My Cid*, from
the mid-12th century, the oldest of a number of epic poems relating the feats of
the 11th-century Spanish knight Rodrigo de Bivar (Rui Dias) (*c.*1040–99).
ZHIGULYOVSKOE, MARTOVSKOE, ADMIRALTY: brands of bottled beer.
GAUDI: Antonio (Gaudì-i-Cornet): a Spanish architect (1852–1926) who
worked in Barcelona.
AND WHACKED IT LIKE A SWORD: the epic poem describes five different
ways of opening bottles of beer.

Page 36
A BLOODSHOT HOOP DRIFTED ABOVE THE PALLID TOWN: could this

perhaps be a solar eclipse?

Page 39
BELOMOR: Belomor Canal *papyroses* (vern.).
BALDA: a character in Pushkin's story *A Tale of a Priest and His Worker Balda* (1830).

Page 41
DRANK DOWN THE MIX: in Russia this kind of cocktail is popularly known as "yorsh".

Page 42
FINITA LA TRAGEDIA (Italian): "The tragedy is over".
AWAKENING, THE SUN OF RUSSIA: illustrated magazines published in St Petersburg in the early 20th century. The magazine *Ogonyok* was similar until 1985.

Page 45
BLOW-UP: 1. to arise, appear; 2. an outburst of irritation, a scandal 3. A photographic enlargement (Appendix to the *Large English-Russian Dictionary* edited by I.R. Galperin, pub. Russky Yazyk, Moscow 1981).
BLOW-UP (photographic enlargement): the title of a film by the Italian director Michelangelo Antonioni (1967, Great Britain, Grand Prix at the Cannes International Film Festival). The film shows the artist striving to depict unadorned reality and present the factual truth of reportage. The final scene of the film shows the process of the creation of almost material reality through a thought game; win the game and reality is changed. The story *Blow-Up* describes a similar process.
PANTHEISM: (Greek "pan", meaning "everything", and "theos", meaning "god"): religious and philosophical teachings that identify God with the totality of the world.

Page 47
THE MECHANICAL: Ilya Davidovich Kobot works at the All-Union Order of the Red Labour Banner Scientific Research and Design Institute for the Mechanical Processing of Useful Minerals at 199026 Leningrad, Vasilievsky Island, Line 21, Building 8a.

Page 50
COLONEL ZORIN'S STORY: a film by the director A.A. Bobrovsky, Mosfilm Studios, 1979 (this detail allows us to date the action to 1979 or 1980).

Page 54
ACROSS HIS BLUE UNIFORM: a patent anachronism, since the Soviet militia changed from blue to grey uniforms long before the time of the action in the story *Blow-Up* (approximately 1970).

Page 55
RINALDO RINALDINI: an Italian bandit.

Page 57
DEMIS ROUSSOS: a Greek singer. To judge from the number of pictures of him in evidence at the time, the most popular person in Leningrad in the late 1970s.
WHY IN HELL'S NAME: as a true pupil of Maxim, Pyotr repeats his teacher's phrase precisely.
THE BRONZE HORSEMAN: the statue of Peter the Great in Leningrad by the sculptor Etienne Falconet (1778).

Page 58
ANTHROPOSOPHY: (Greek "anthropos", meaning "man", and "sophia", meaning "wisdom"): a decadent mystical teaching, a variety of theosophy. The system of anthroposophy focuses on the deified human essence, which is accessible only to the initiated. Anthroposophy was founded by the German occultist Rudolph Steiner (1861–1925).
ALCONAUT (vern. from "alcohol" and the Greek "nautes", meaning a mariner): an alcoholic; the same as "wino".

Page 59
ELLINGTON, Edward ("Duke") (1899–1974): an American jazz pianist and composer, the creator of various styles of jazz.
THE BEATLES: a world-famous English rock group (1959–70), comprising John Lennon, Paul McCartney, George Harrison and Ringo Starr.

Page 60
LAMAISM (from the Tibetan "lama"): one of the main branches of Buddhism, which developed in the 12th to 14th centuries in Tibet on the basis of Mahayana Buddhism and Tantrism, with elements of the Bon-Po religion. The major religion followed by Tibetans, Buryats and Tuvinians. Lamaism accepts all the basic dogmas of Buddhism and ascribes a special role in salvation to lamas.

Page 65
SHESTOV, Lev Isaakovich (real name Shvartsman, 1866–1938): a Russian religious philosopher and writer. Lived in emigration from 1920. Close to the teachings of Kierkegaard. A critic of rationalism in philosophy, ethics and theology. Acknowledged the absurdity of life and mystic faith as a means to salvation. In Shestov's opinion science and reason investigate that which is of least value for the individual as a unique personality.
LOTUS-EATER: here, an individual who is "crazy" about ("hooked" on) Eastern thought and philosophy.

Page 66
McCARTNEY (Paul McCartney, born 1942): an English rock musician.
IVANOVA, Tatiana: a contemporary French singer.

Page 67

GO SI: (*c*.1025–*c*.1100): a famous Chinese landscape painter who is regarded as having consummated the monumental landscape tradition of the 10 th and 11th centuries.

GO SI WROTE: this is inaccurate. The words quoted by Pyotr belong to Go Sy, the artist's son, who collected together Go Si's utterances on the art of painting after his father's death. The son wrote the introduction and the concluding section of the book: "In those days when my father would take up the brush, he would always sit without fail at a clean desk by a bright window, light the incense, take his best brush and excellent ink, wash his hands and clean his inkwell. It was as though he were receiving a great guest. His spirit was pure, his thoughts were focused. Then he would begin working."

Go Si's tract "On the exalted essence of forests and streams" in an anthology by Yui An-lan. Peking, 1950 (in Chinese, Russian translation by K. Samosiuk).

THE RENAISSANCE: a period in the cultural and ideological development of the countries of Western and Central Europe (in Italy, the 14th to 16th centuries, in other countries the late 15th and 16th centuries), representing the transition from medieval culture to the culture of modern times. A humanistic world-view, an appeal to the cultural heritage of antiquity and its "renaissance".

During the Renaissance the philosophical ideas of neo-Platonism and pantheism became widespread (see note to page 45).

Page 68

FAST: a religious prohibition on the taking of certain kinds of food or food in general. A means of purifying and revivifying the human soul. During a fast participation in any kind of profane festivity is prohibited.

IF YOU BUT KNEW: an inaccurate citation of Anna Akhmatova's poem "I have no need of an odic host" (1936) from the cycle *Craft Secrets*.

If you but knew from what litter
Verses do spring, no shame knowing,
Like yellow dandelions by the fence,
Like goosefoot and coarse burdock growing.

Page 69

RIGHT, SO . . . JUST A MOMENT: Vasilii's narrative is reminiscent of the legend of Doctor Faustus (Faust).

Page 72

METROPOLITAN ANTONII: Antonii Blium, a contemporary metropolitan of the Russian Orthodox Church.

SAMSARA (Sanskrit, "wandering"): in Hinduism and Buddhism the concept of a chain of transitions from one corporeal integument to another, the cycle of births and deaths. The transmigration of souls proceeds in accordance with the law of karma (retribution).

SUCCUBUS: a female demon in Western European mythology. An incubus is a male demon of the same kind. A species of living dead which is in the habit of marrying the living.

CYNIC: a follower of the ancient Greek philosopher Antisphenes, the founder of the cynical school. The best-known of the cynics is Diogenes of Sinope. The cynics believed that happiness and virtue could only be achieved by abandoning the benefits of civilisation and sensual pleasures. They disdained the accepted norms of society and religious cults.

MAINZ: a city in Germany on the river Rhine, well-known in ancient times.

HOLSTINIA: the Russian name for the principality of Holstein (so-called from the 11th century). Since 1949 Schleswig-Holstein has been a "land", or administrative unit, in the Federal Republic of Germany; it has a territory of 15,700 square kilometres and a population of 2.6 million (1978); its administrative centre is the city of Kiel.

PANNONIA: a Roman province established in the 8th century BC, which occupied part of the territory of modern Hungary, Austria and Yugoslavia. Its name was derived from the Illyrian tribes that populated it, the Pannonians.

Page 73

SAVATTHI, DJETTAVAN: cities in India.

SANDWICH ISLANDS (Hawaiian Islands): an archipelago in the Pacific Ocean consisting of 24 islands, the peaks of a chain of underwater volcanoes, covered in damp tropical forest. A US holiday resort.

OREKHOVO-ZUEVO: a town (since 1917) in the Moscow Region located on the river Klyazma, a very old centre of the cotton fabric industry.

MEPHISTOPHELES (German, also Mephisto): the devil, the image of that spirit in the folklore of the peoples of Europe, a character in Goethe's *Faust* and other works of literature.

PRIEN: an ancient town on the western seaboard of Asia Minor, which originated in the 11th century BC and flourished during the 4th to 1st centuries BC. Remains of public buildings, shrines and fortifications are visible today.

BIANT: "The son of Tevtam of Prien, whom Satyr regards as the first among the seven. Some say he is a rich man, but Durid says quite the opposite, that he is a sponger." (Diogenes of Laert, *On the Lives, Teachings and Utterances of the Philosophers.*)

THEBES: an ancient greek City in Beothia, the centre of the Boeotian League of Greek cities (6th–4th centuries BC).

PLATO (427–347 BC): an ancient Greek philosopher, a pupil of Socrates.

Page 74

WESTERNISER: a member of a movement in Russian social thought of the mid-19th century. The Westernisers were in favour of Russia's development along Western European lines and were opposed to the Slavophiles.

FAUST: a hero of German folk-legend and world literature, a symbol of the passionate desire for knowledge. His prototype was Doctor Johannes Faust (1480?–1540?), an astrologist. The story of Faust's pact with the devil is first

told in the German folk book *The History of Doctor Faust, the Well-Known Magician and Sorcerer* (1587).
LOTMAN, Yu.M. (1922–93): a Soviet literary scholar who studied culture in its historical and philosophical context.
BAKHTIN, M.M. (1895–1975): a Soviet literary scholar and art theorist (*Problems of Dostoevsky's Poetics*, Moscow, 1979).

Page 76
THE HUBBUB FADED: a poem by Boris Pasternak (1890–1960).
FROM THE ISLAND: a Russian folk song ("Stenka Razin").
AND HAVING TROD THE PATH OF LIFE HALFWAY: Dante Alighieri (1265–1325), *The Divine Comedy*, Russian translation by M.L. Lozinsky (1866–1955).

Page 79
PUSHKIN: a town in the Leningrad Region (until 1918 Tsarskoe Selo; thereafter until 1937 Detskoe Selo). A palace and park estate of the 18th and 19th centuries.
MENSHIKOV IN THAT PICTURE BY SURIKOV: a reference to the picture *Menshikov at Beryozovo* (1883) by the Russian artist V.I. Surikov (1848–1916).

Page 80
NIGHT-FEEDER: the name Plato gave to Diogenes because he lived in a barrel without any window or source of light. This fact is apparently stated by Diogenes of Laert in the book *On the Lives, Teachings and Utterances of the Famous Philosophers* (Mysl Publishers, Moscow, 1979).

Page 82
BIBILIOPHILE: a well-known shop in Leningrad which dealt in old and second-hand books (59 Liteiny Prospect).

Page 86
HERACLES (Hercules): a hero of Greek mythology, the son of Zeus. Endowed with exceptional strength, he performed numerous great feats. A well-known cycle of stories relates the twelve labours of Heracles.
VITEBSK STATION: a mainline railway station in Leningrad. The first station in Russia and the starting point of the country's first railway line.
LONG STREAK OF PSEUDO-PELAGIAN SHIT: Maxim is hinting at the closeness of Pyotr's views to the so-called Pelagian heresy.
PELAGIANISM: in opposition to the concept of grace and predetermination of St Augustine, the teaching of the Christian monk Pelagius (*c.*60–*post* 418) emphasised the moral and ascetic efforts of the individual, denying the hereditary power of sin. It was denounced as heresy at the first Ecumenical Council in 431. Pelagianism is typical of Pyotr in general: "Everything is possible for man, and so forth" and "As we wish, so shall we do" are

utterances by Pyotr which express the essential content of the Pelagian heresy.

Page 89
THE LITERARY GAZETTE: an organ of the governing body of the Union of
Writers of the USSR. Published since 1929. Since 1967 a weekly (16 pages).
Deals with questions of literature, art, society and politics, economics,
sociology, morality, ecology, history and other problems. (The Voice of America
has described *The Literary Gazette* as "a Soviet weekly for the intelligentsia".)

Page 90
BAUDELAIRE, Charles (1821–67): a French poet and forerunner of French
symbolism.
THE HERMITAGE: a museum in Leningrad, one of the largest museums of
art, culture and history in the world. Founded in 1764 as the private collection
of Catherine II (the Great). First opened to the public in 1852. An outstanding
architectural ensemble.

Page 91
PORTRAIT OF JEREMIAH DECKER: a portrait by the Dutch artist
Rembrandt Harmensz van Rijn (1606–69).

Page 92
VIVEKANANDA, Swami (1863–1902): an Indian humanist thinker, religious
and social reformer.
DUALISM: a philosophical teaching based on the recognition of two equally
important principles – spirit and matter. The greatest proponent of dualism is
René Descartes.
I DON'T WANT A MILLION: Pyotr's words recall those of Dmitry
Karamazov in Dostoevsky's novel *The Brothers Karamazov*.

Page 93
GET A SMALL ONE: the reference is to a small (0.25 litres) mug of beer at a
kiosk, for a price of 11 kopecks.
VONNEGUT, Kurt (born 1922): an American writer who employs the devices
of grotesque and fabulist literature in his works.
INDULGENCE: in the Roman Catholic church the forgiveness of sins and also
a document in confirmation of this.
TWO FORTY-TWO, FOUR TWENTY: two roubles 42 kopecks and four
roubles 20 kopecks were the prices of fortified wine (in 0.7 litre bottles) and
vodka (0.5 litre) respectively in 1980.
GRACE: in religious terms a specific heavenly power sent down to man from
above in order to overcome his essential inner sinfulness and allow him to
attain salvation.

Page 94
ASPIRIN (*Acidum acetylsalicylicum*): an ester of acetic acid (vinegar). Exerts an

antipyretic, analgesic and anti-inflammatory effect.

Page 95

BARBAMIL (*Barbamilum*): 5-ethyl-5-isoamylbarbiturate of sodium. Exerts a soporific, relaxing and antispasmodic effect. Used in cases of insomnia, epilepsy and excitation.

DRAUGHT'S CHEAPER: the reference is to draught beer.

Page 101

APOCRYPHA (Greek, "concealed", "secret"): early Christian writings not included in the biblical canon.

PLAYS: for the most part the titles of these plays represent unrealised projects of V. Shinkarev or his friends.

BAKUNIN, M.A. (1814–76): a Russian revolutionary and theoretician of anarchism, one of the ideologists of the revolutionary *narodnik* movement.

ABBA: a rock group popular in the early 1980s. The name is composed of the first letters of the names of the members of the quartet.

BONEY M: a black West German rock group, popular in the late 1970s, who sang in English.

Page 102

THE GERMAN IDEOLOGY: a joint work by Karl Marx and Friedrich Engels, in which they expounded the materialist conception of history. Written in 1845–6 and first published in 1932 in the USSR, the *German Ideology* expounds the concepts of social-economic formation and the state as an instrument of economic domination by a class.

Page 104

THUS SPAKE MAXIM: this chapter is a stylistic imitation of *Thus Spake Zarathustra* (1883–4), a major work by the German philosopher Friedrich Nietzsche (1844–1900).

FASTFOOT (or "footman"): a Leningrad shoe factory founded in 1962 which produced various types of low-quality and uncomfortable footwear.

HEMLOCK: a species of perennial bog grass from the umbellate family, poisonous. Socrates was condemned to die by poisoning with the juice of hemlock.

Page 105

WALSINGHAM: a character in Pushkin's play *A Feast in Time of Plague* (1830).

VENYA: a character in Venedikt Erofeev's work *Moscow-Petushki*.

Page 106

MAXIM AND FYODOR: THE CORRESPONDENCE: Fyodor's aim is to create works similar to Dostoevsky's *Writer's Diary* and Gogol's *Correspondence With Friends*.

OZHOGIN VOLOCHOK: a village in the Batetsk district of the Novgorod Region.

Page 110
AS THE GREAT CLASSIC WROTE: the classic referred to here is Venedikt Erofeev, a contemporary Soviet Russian writer whose best-known work is *Moscow-Petushki*.

Page 114
AUTOPILOT: the condition in which absolute drunkenness has not yet given way to sleep.
8 MARCH: International Women's Day, in the USSR a public holiday.

Page 115
SNOUT-TWISTER: vodka, primarily cheap varieties of local manufacture.

Page 116
PORT: naturally, not from Portugal.

SHORT STORIES

THE TAME HEDGEHOG

THE TAME HEDGEHOG

Everybody knows that hedgehogs are woodland creatures. Of course, there are desert hedgehogs and steppe hedgehogs and some kind of long-eared hedgehog, but I don't know about those. In any case, hedgehogs are not domestic creatures. If you bring a hedgehog home from the woods and keep it over the winter, you can't take it back to the woods in the summer; it becomes tame and grows unused to the wild life, so full of dangers.

One tame hedgehog became ill and his owners took him to the hospital in their car. He spent a long time there while he was ill, a whole year, and when he got well it turned out there was nowhere to discharge him to: his owners had moved to a different flat and forgotten all about the hedgehog; they didn't visit him or bring in parcels for him. And he couldn't go back to the woods any more – who could possibly live in the woods after such a long illness?

There was nothing else for him to do but carry on living in the hospital. All the doctors and nurses were actually glad that he stayed with them – the hedgehog was kind and he knew how to do lots of things; he decorated the wards with pictures that he drew himself and he cut fancy chains out of coloured paper.

Some of his friends at the hospital felt sorry for the hedgehog because he had nowhere to live, but the hedgehog didn't feel at all unhappy. He helped the nurses and pushed the patients in their wheelchairs and he always had paints, brushes and paper in his locker for drawing with. Everybody loved the hedgehog and so nobody was surprised when a cat asked him to move in with her.

Cats are domestic animals. They always have a home of their own. There are wild cats too – cats who walk on their own, but to be honest they are rather nasty and stupid animals.

A domestic cat is a beautiful and clever animal that loves its home, and if it turns wild and begins to walk on its own, then it becomes something worse than a wild cat – a garbage-heap cat.

The hedgehog loved the cat a lot too; nobody else was so affectionate with him or purred so beautifully. The cat's fur was soft and warm, not like the hedgehog's prickles. The cat smelled of milk, which hedgehogs love as much as cats do.

The cat and the hedgehog began living together and they were happy – the cat even liked the fact that the hedgehog had prickly fur that took a whole hour to smooth out, and the fact that he rustled loudly at night (hedgehogs do have one bad habit – they don't go to bed until late and in the meantime they roam about all over the place).

The cat bought the hedgehog a coat and felt boots. In the mornings they went for a walk in the park together or to the cinema.

In the afternoons the cat tidied up the house and cooked dinner, and the hedgehog collected potatoes or decorated the house with his pictures. The cat liked these pictures so much that she didn't like it when the hedgehog took one or two of them to his old friends at the hospital.

In the evenings they told each other about everything that had happened to them during the day, played draughts or simply ran around the house singing a song: "What a lovely pussy cat our prickly little hedgehog has!"

Then the cat went to bed and the hedgehog roamed around for a while. The cat lay there listening to the hedgehog eating potatoes in the kitchen or drawing and she felt calm and peaceful; she folded down her ears and went to sleep.

In the summer time they went out into the country on the train and looked at the woods the hedgehog used to live in when he was wild. The cat snorted, she couldn't understand how anyone could live in the woods. The hedgehog laughed, but he felt a bit sad.

They lived like that for a long time and they thought they would be happy until they grew old; he would become an old hedgehog and she would become an old cat, and they would still go for walks together, only with sticks.

But one year there was a very hot, stifling summer and then a damp, cold autumn, and the cat became flighty. She was far too

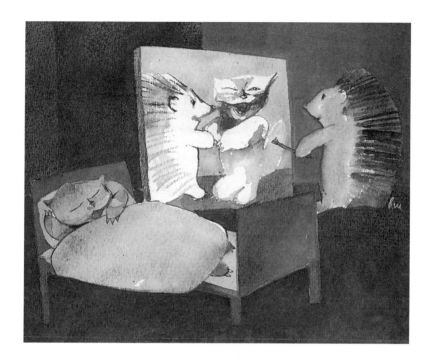

spoiled, and she began to think the hedgehog was too prickly and not like a cat, and she ought to be friends with an animal like a cat – beautiful, fluffy and playful. And she got to know an animal like that.

And in the winter this is what the cat did: she told the hedgehog that she was going away on business, dressed the hedgehog in his felt boots and coat and took him back to the hospital.

At first the hedgehog didn't realise that he was being left in the hospital again and he waited calmly for the cat. During the first few days the cat phoned the hospital and asked if the hedgehog was all right, if he'd made any new friends and whether he had enough to eat.

One of the nurses said to him that the cat was probably going to leave him in the hospital forever and wasn't going to live with him any more: she'd made friends with a ferret who was funny, fluffy and playful.

The hedgehog thought the nurse was joking and laughing at

him; he laughed himself and said the cat would come back soon from her business trip and collect him and they would live together happily again – the cat would do the housework and cook the dinner, and the hedgehog would collect potatoes and decorate the house. The nurse felt sorry for the hedgehog and she didn't tell him that the cat had abandoned him. But the hedgehog already realised that she had.

* * *

A dog used to come to the hospital to visit her sick son, walk with him in the yard and read books to him. The dog lived in the same building as the cat and she knew the hedgehog and his story very well; she brought him gifts of oranges and apples, and brought paints and a brush so that the hedgehog could decorate the hospital again with his pictures and paper chains.

But the hedgehog didn't draw any more. Usually he just sat on his bed without speaking. He thanked the dog for the fruit, of course, but he ate hardly any of it.

One day the dog told him it was the cat who had sent him the oranges. The dog had wanted to cheer the hedgehog up, but he wouldn't take any of the oranges and even asked her to take the coat and felt boots back to the cat.

The dog was very upset and didn't know what she ought to do. She remembered how jolly the hedgehog used to be, how many friends he used to have and how much everybody used to loved him.

Now the hedgehog didn't have any new friends in the hospital; he just sat there and said nothing, he didn't play with anybody. When he was happy everybody loved him, but when he was unhappy they stopped loving him.

But the cat was unhappy too, and nobody loved her any more. She began to miss the hedgehog, their conversations and their songs; she looked at the pictures he'd left behind and cried. The ferret got angry with her and threw the pictures about. All the ferret knew how to do was laugh and boast.

They soon ate up all the potatoes the hedgehog had collected. The ferret wandered around the house a bit, yawned a bit and ran away from the cat to go robbing and killing. For the ferret was a bandit – he used to lie in wait for chickens on the road, and actually kill them and eat them up. The cat was left to live on her own. Every evening she called on the dog and asked all about the hedgehog, but all the dog could tell her was that the hedgehog just sat there and never said anything.

The cat came back home and went to bed, but she couldn't get to sleep for a long time; she remembered how she used to fall asleep before, when the hedgehog used to eat potatoes in the kitchen and rustle his brushes, and everything was peaceful and happy, and in the morning they used to wake up and go for walks in the park.

The cat came to the hospital during the time for walks and watched the hedgehog walking in the yard in a hospital coat and felt boots. The cat wanted to talk to the hedgehog and ask him to forgive her;

she wanted him to come back, but she was ashamed. She could see that the hedgehog noticed her, but he didn't go across to her. And after that he stopped coming out for walks altogether.

Then the cat couldn't stand it any more. She rushed into the hospital to see the hedgehog and said: "Dear hedgehog, forgive me, please! Come back to live with me! You're nice, and the ferret's nasty!"

The hedgehog asked: "What if the ferret had turned out better, would you have forgotten about me?"

"Hedgehog, for me you're the very best in all the world."

The hedgehog thought a bit and said: "How can I come and live with you again? How could we be so happy, run around and sing songs? I'd be afraid you might meet some other fine animal and put me in the hospital again."

Then the hospital bell rang for the end of visiting hours and the nurses began chasing all the visitors out. The dog left her sick son, but they didn't chase the cat out.

The hedgehog still didn't say anything; then he said goodbye and went back to his ward. They put the light out in the corridor and the cat went home. She felt very sad and she cried, but she still believed the hedgehog would think things over, forgive her and come back to her.

The next day she got up early, cleaned and tidied everything in the flat, made a delicious dinner and began to wait for the hedgehog.

Please do forgive her, hedgehog, we all want you to!

——————— CUT OFF HERE FOR CHILDREN ———————
(An alternative ending, the way Leo Tolstoy does it)

She cleaned and tidied everything in the flat, made a delicious dinner and began to wait for the hedgehog.

But the hedgehog didn't come that day, or the next day. The hedgehog took to drink and he died under a hedge.

And the cat started living with some Ussurian street rat *(Hyppophtalmichtys molitrix ussuriensis)*.

1987

THE KING
OF THE BEASTS

THE KING OF THE BEASTS

In the middle of the Jordanian desert, not very far from the strange Dead Sea, there stands a fortified monastery of stone. This is the Monastery of St Jerome, one of the most ancient in Palestine.

The monks give all the pilgrims who come here a little icon and feed them with bread. It is simple hospitality, but very hard to forget. There are not many places where it is possible to taste such delicious bread.

There are no secrets to the recipe – it is simply that any food is delicious if it is prepared with a prayer. And this bread is almost the only thing the monks eat, which is the way it has been for fifteen centuries – the rule was established by the founder of the monastery, the venerable St Jerome. He is also shown on the little icon: a wise old monk standing in the desert, with a lion lying at his feet.

The lion is a dangerous and unpredictable beast and any attempt to tame it always ends badly. Of course, there are trained lions who have been weakened and are compelled through force and cruelty to perform various tricks, but if the lion-tamer had no whip and revolver things would go badly with him.

In the presence of saints, though, many things in the world change, not just people's characters, but even the very laws of nature. The prayer of a saint can bring about a miracle. If fact, even our prayers can.

This is what I discovered about the lion who is shown beside St Jerome on the icon.

* * *

One day the venerable Jerome was walking through the desert when he saw a lion right in front of him. The wise monk prepared himself to face death, but the lion was not lying in wait for him in order to eat him up. He lifted up his paw and Jerome could see that the lion

was hurt: his paw was all swollen from a large thorn that had pene-
trated deep into it. There are many such sharp thorns in the desert;
many of the plants have them instead of leaves in order to conserve
as much moisture as possible.

The lion was suffering such torment that he had decided to ask a
man for help. Seeing him in such misery, Jerome carefully pulled out
the thorn, washed the wound with wine and water, and bound it up
with his kerchief. The lion immediately felt better, and when Jerome
set off on his way to the monastery, the lion followed him, he felt so
very grateful to the saint for healing him.

"Where are you going?" asked Jerome. "I am a monk, and you are
the king of the beasts. Go to your desert, I am going to the
monastery."

But the lion did not obey him and kept walking after him, limping
slightly.

"Surely you don't want to go to the monastery?" said the wise
monk. "Life in the monastery is hard: the monks only eat boiled food
once every month. I suppose you don't eat boiled food anyway, but
we eat nothing except bread, roots and dates, and is that really possible with your nature? The most important business of monks is
prayer. We pray for all the people and in that way we protect them.
Some of us do penance, many of us work, weaving baskets out of
date-palm branches but what will you be able to do?"

All the way back to the monastery Jerome tried to persuade the lion
to go back to the desert, but all in vain, it was clear that the lion had
decided to remain faithful to the wise old monk.

And so the two of them entered the monastery together. The monks
who happened to be in the courtyard scattered and ran, but before
they became really terrified, Jerome said.

"Do not be frightened, brothers, this is a gentle and rational
beast!"

"Why did you bring him here, Father Jerome?" the monks asked,
trying to keep their distance.

"He himself wished to come to the monastery and remain here."

"Father Jerome, surely a wild beast cannot be a monk! A beast has no immortal soul, he should not even enter a church. Only foolish children will bring a cat to church to the priest, saying he is so clever and kind, he must be baptised to make him an Orthodox cat."

Jerome glanced at the lion, who was standing silently with his eyes lowered. Indeed, how could a lion serve the Lord? Except perhaps by observing the vow of silence.

"Truly, my brothers," said the venerable Jerome, "Christ came to save people. Beasts do not have an immortal soul. They are a part of nature and it is people's responsibility to care for nature. So let us care for the lion, since he wishes to be one of our novices. Let him guard the ass."

The monks immediately agreed with their wise elder about this. For the monastery had an ass that carried water from the holy river Jordan, and it was no easy job to pasture him, since it is very hot in the Jordanian desert.

Jerome taught the lion what to do and every day the lion pastured the ass: he took its bridle in his jaws and led it out into the desert to a little meadow where grass grew. The ass nibbled away the grass and the lion moved it to another little meadow.

Of course, such meek behaviour is amazing for a lion. Like all the monks, he lived on bread and roots, although the lion is a carnivorous animal and it is harder for him to bear hunger than it is for people. The walls of a lion's stomach are lined with little spikes, and when his stomach is empty the spikes prick him.

Whenever the lion had a free minute he would run to the wise old monk and lie at his feet. The venerable Jerome would read the Psalter and the lion thought thoughts of his own.

Now, one day at the height of summer the weather became really oppressive. Down by the Dead Sea in summer the temperature often climbs to over 50 degrees – it is hard to think properly in such heat and during the day people stay at home.

Early in the morning the ass carried some water from the Jordan to the monastery, then the lion led it to a little meadow, crept into the shade of a burdock plant and fell asleep there, completely exhausted from the heat.

Just at that time a caravan happened to be travelling across the desert to Egypt for wheat. The merchants saw the ass wandering about all alone. The caravan drivers looked everywhere round about and searched for the owner of the ass, but they did not notice the lion under the burdock, or perhaps the ass had already wandered a long way. What sense was there in leaving an abandoned ass in the desert? They tied its bridle to a camel and took it with them to Egypt.

When the lion woke up the ass was gone!

The caravan was a thin line on the far distant horizon, moving away towards Egypt, but the line could not be seen through the shimmering haze of the Dead Sea.

The lion went dashing off to look for the ass, racing around the desert and glancing into every bush; he even ran to the river Jordan, but all in vain – the ass had vanished into thin air. The only possibility left was that it had gone back to the monastery on its own, and when the sun was already setting the lion ran back there.

The monks saw the lion enter the monastery alone, looking dejected.

"Aha!" they shouted. "Everything's clear now! Eaten the ass, have you? A fine novice: he's gobbled up our poor little ass!"

When the lion realised that the ass had not come back to the monastery, he hung his head even lower.

The venerable Jerome came out into the courtyard.

"Where is the ass? Have you really eaten him?"

The lion could not prove his innocence (even if he could have spoken); he did not understand it himself – all he could do was stare sadly at the ground.

"Now what is to be done?" said Jerome. "Clearly it is not in your nature to live on bread and roots, we were wrong to torment you. Go back to the desert."

The lion raised his eyes, and I do not know what Jerome read in that glance, hurt feelings or love, but the wise old monk realised that the lion would never leave him.

"As you wish, but no grumbling – now you will do for the monastery what the ass used to do."

And from that moment the lion's life was one of drudgery.

It is one thing to pasture an ass, even though it may be hot and boring work, but it is quite another for a noble beast to lug a barrel of water through the desert.

They loaded a barrel the size of four waterskins on to the lion's back, which was not adapted for carrying heavy loads, and he walked (on soft paws, not hooves) from the river to the monastery. But this work did have one advantage – once he had brought the water he was free, and so now the lion could spend more time with Father Jerome.

Everyone who visited the monastery marvelled at the lion and pitied him, especially one old soldier who had come to the monastery to pray.

"Does your lion have a name?" the old soldier asked the monks.

"We have begun to call him Jordan, because he brings us water from the river Jordan."

"How were you able to force a proud lion to carry out work so unfitted to him?"

"Nobody compelled him, it was his own wish to become a novice. He follows Father Jerome around like a pupil. Clearly, the power of our elder's righteousness is very great, if it has subdued and bound to itself a wild beast. In truth, Jordan shows us how the beasts were obedient to Adam before his fall and expulsion from paradise."

"He may well wish to be a novice, but surely he does not wish to carry a barrel on his back?"

"That is entirely Jordan's own fault: he ate the ass which brought us our water. That is why he bears it without whinging. He knows he has sinned and wishes to make atonement."

"What a meek and humble soul! I am no better than a crocodile compared to him!" exclaimed the soldier. "You know, brothers, you should have pity on Jordan. See how thin he has become!"

"That is not the worse thing," the monks replied. "We feel even more sorry for the lion because Father Jerome is very old, he will leave us and go to the Lord, but Jordan, having no immortal soul, will lose him forever and be inconsolable."

"I will tell you what we can do," the soldier suggested. "When I receive my pension soon I will buy a new ass for three pieces of gold and give it to the monastery."

In the meantime the merchant from Arabia who had taken the ass to Egypt was returning to Jerusalem to sell his wheat. He was following the same route, and while the lion had been unlucky at their first encounter (although the lion did not know this, because he had been asleep), he was fortunate enough to notice the caravan on its return. That is not really surprising, since after all lions have much keener vision than people.

Jordan was actually on his way back from the river with his barrel, stepping carefully in order not to stand on a thorn with his full weight. Suddenly he raised his head and saw the caravan, and with it his lost ass. The lion dashed forward with a cry of joy, and the caravan drivers saw a strange and incomprehensible sight: a roaring lion dashing straight at them with a barrel on its back.

Of course, without pausing for thought the merchants scattered in all directions, and Jordan could easily have taken all the camels and the wheat. But the lion did not want what was not his. He took the bridle of his ass in his mouth and led it back to the monastery, constantly looking round and snarling something.

Well, you can imagine what happened at the monastery when the lion entered the courtyard, beaming with joy, followed by the ass! The monks embraced Jordan and kissed him, said "Forgive us, Jordan", and petted the ass, but they never did find out where he had disappeared to for so long to return so well-fed and well groomed.

"Forgive us, Jordan!" said Father Jerome. "The truth of everything is revealed, but it is good that we have discovered it in this life. You have borne insult and tolerated with dignity a punishment that you did not deserve. It is a rare thing even for a man to trust so completely in the will of God – you truly are the King of the Beasts!"

NOTES FOR ENGLISH READERS

by Andrew Bromfield

The author's own notes translated from the Russian (pages 119–32) are effectively part of the original text, and should be read in that spirit.

These simple notes for the English reader are intended merely to point up significant elements of the Soviet context in which *Maxim and Fyodor* was written. Readers who are familiar with that context can safely ignore them.

For the sake of convenience, all the notes refer in the past tense to a Soviet Russian society which is now receding into history. However, this should not be taken to imply that everything in Russia has changed!

THOUGHTS
Page 13
the philosophy of Marxism
Under the Soviet system the materialist philosophy of Marxism, in the guise of Marxism-Leninism, was the official ideology of the state. It was formally regarded as the only objective world-view that defined the fundamental principles of all social and scientific thought.

that other place
A reference to the Soviet secret police or KGB calling Maxim in for an interview.

Page 14
the second bottle of port
In Soviet times fortified "port wine" (made in Russia, not Portugal) was a favourite beverage among Russian alcoholics and others who consumed cheap alcohol.

one of those [books] that are best not discussed with people you don't know very well

The censor was active throughout the Soviet period, and books with "dissident", "subversive" or "anti-Marxist" contents were always repressed with a greater or lesser degree of zeal.

Nekrasov
Nikolai Nekrasov (1821–77/78) was a Russian writer whose folk-oriented poetry expressed sentiments which nourished the developing movement for social reform or revolution.

Page 15
beer is made up of atoms
A comical hint at the simplistic exposition of Marx's materialism by his colleague Engels (see the tongue-in-cheek note in the original text).

He who does not work, neither shall he eat
Another reference to Marxism. The Soviet Union was supposedly developing from the condition of socialism which, according to Marx, operated on the principle "from each according to their ability, to each according to their contribution", to communism, under which the principle "from each according to their ability, to each according to their needs" would apply.

THERE AND BACK AGAIN
Page 25
Fyodor handed in the jar
In Soviet Russia empty bottles and glass jars from alcoholic drinks and various food products (known collectively as "steklotara" or "glass packaging") could be handed in at special collection points for a few kopecks each. This was one way to obtain the money for the next drink.

The other people in the flat
In Soviet Russia communal flats of
various sizes with shared kitchen
and bathroom facilities dated back
to the early post-revolutionary
days. Even now not every family in
Moscow and St Petersburg lives in
self-contained accommodation.
Various details in *Maxim and
Fyodor* illustrate the conditions of
life in such flats.

housing management office
The local municipal agency
responsible for the maintenance of
public housing and related services.
Almost all housing was publicly
owned in Soviet times. Flats have
since been privatised.

the people's court
The lowest level of the judicial
system established in Russia after
the Revolution of 1917.

the beer stall
Street kiosks dealing in one
particular type of goods (of which
the supply might often be irregular)
were a distinctive feature of the
Soviet retail system. Beer stalls
were perennially popular – but
even they could run out of beer.

MAXIM MONOGATARI
Pages 27/29
*the Vodka and Spirits shop/the
Delicatessen*
Under the Soviet system the entire
economy was run by the state.
Many shops had no other names
but the type (not brand) of goods
that they sold. The signs on
their façades read simply
"Footwear", "Bread", "Books",
"Cheese", etc.

FOR THE PEOPLE'S CAUSE
Page 32
padded jackets
Padded jackets were standard wear
for workers on building sites, in
factories, collective farms etc. – and
also in the Soviet prison camps.

Page 33
underground activists
These are members of the
revolutionary movement that
led to the establishment of the
Soviet state.

THE LAY OF MY MAXIM
Pages 34–40
*whacked it like a sword/flicked the
cap off with his nail/the cap clenched
in his teeth/linked them and pulled*
"Serious" drinkers in Soviet Russia
took great pride in their skill in
opening bottles (with metal caps or
plastic stoppers) without using any
instrument.

BLOW-UP
Page 45
Soviet Encyclopedic Dictionary
Pantheism would in principle be
regarded as an un-Soviet and un-
Marxist concept. (However, the
1981 edition of the *Soviet
Encyclopaedic Dictionary* does
contain an entry on it!)

a militiaman standing in the doorway
The ordinary (not secret or
military) police in Soviet Russia
were known as the militia.

Page 47
Puzhaty lit the gas on his ring
In a communal flat each resident
would have his or her own ring on
the cooker.

Page 50
a hostile element
A reference to the Soviet regime's historical obsession with possible opposition to the state and its doctrine from hostile or alien "class elements".

VISITORS
Page 57
Bronze Horseman
A famous equestrian statue of Peter the Great in St Petersburg, made by the French sculptor Falconet.

Pages 57–8
Trying to paint pictures is just a waste of time
In Soviet times it was common for creative artists who did not conform to the official doctrines of "socialist realism" to support themselves by working as yard-keepers, labourers, etc.

Page 73
you Westerniser
In the 19th century the debate on Russia's future focused on the whether the country should follow a "Western" or a "Slavic" path. The two main schools of thought were known as "Westernisers" and "Slavophiles".

Page 76
The hubbub faded
This verse is from one of Boris Pasternak's poems in the appendix to his novel *Doctor Zhivago*.

From the island to the channel
This is verse from the well-known Russian song "Stenka Razin", about a 17th-century brigand who defied the authority of Tsar Alexei

Mikhailovich and was eventually condemned to death and quartered in Moscow.

cocktail of carbolic/extract of boot-polish
When vodka, beer or wine were unavailable, Soviet drunks would resort to drinking almost anything containing alchohol, frequently poisoning themselves in the process. Eau de cologne was a popular choice.

LET'S GO TO TSARSKOE SELO!
Page 79
Pushkin
Tsarskoe Selo ("Tsar's Village"), near St Petersburg was renamed Pushkin in Soviet times.

Page 81
he'd sell his books on art
In Soviet Russia good books were often in short supply and there were special shops which bought and sold second-hand books at standard prices.

Page 82
Maxim hadn't managed to buy any port
Unpredictable shortages of almost any desirable commodity were a recurrent feature of Soviet life.

The Bibliophile was closed for stocktaking
The managers of Soviet shops were in the habit of closing their premises "for stocktaking" without any advance notice.

a new passport
In Soviet Russia everyone had an internal passport, which was the

fundamental form of identification
for all purposes. A separate passport
was required for foreign travel.

an argument with a speculator
The speculator would have been
selling books privately (and
therefore illegally) at higher prices
than the official ones in the shop.

Page 84
mutual aid fund
A system which allowed people
working in a particular enterprise
or office to borrow small sums to
tide them over until payday.

Page 85
Let's sit in silence
This is a traditional ritual before
anyone takes a long journey.

*Who else could have stopped the
very first taxi*
Soviet taxis were notoriously
difficult to stop.

HANGOVER
Page 89
the army office
As a general rule all men were liable
for conscription into the Soviet
armed forces. Official exceptions
were made for certain categories.

Page 90
"For children crazed with maps"
Extract from Charles Baudelaire's
"The Voyage" from *Flowers of
Evil: a selection*, edited by Marthiel
and Jackson Mathews and
translated by Roy Campbell (New
Directions, New York, 1955).

THUS SPAKE MAXIM
Page 104
New Year trees
In Russia conifer trees are
decorated to celebrate the New
Year rather than Christmas.

**MAXIM AND FYODOR: THE
CORRESPONDENCE**
Page 106
no moonshine either
The habit of producing one's own
hard liquor was widespread in Soviet
Russia, especially in rural areas.

Page 108
no sobering-up station
In Soviet cities drunks on the street
were liable to be picked up by the
militia and taken to special
facilities to sober them up.

Page 111
Yesterday the chairman came round
Rural drunkenness regularly affected
the efficiency of Soviet agriculture.
The chairman of the local collective
farm was a figure with both political
and economic authority.

FYODOR'S DIARY
Page 113
served in Germany
Following the Second World War
the Soviet Union maintained a
military presence in East Germany
(the German Democratic Republic).

Page 114
Tomorrow's 8 March
International Women's Day was
an official public holiday in the
Soviet Union.